THE TAP DANCER

'Andrew Barrow's *The Tap Dancer* . . . must be my favourite novel and one I wish I'd written.'
Alan Bennett

'There's no other novel quite like it. Andrew Barrow has the most curious, in both senses, comic ear and, as if by magic, can turn everyday speech into the stuff of sublime comedy.'
Craig Brown

'Intensely enjoyable – a reward on every page'
Mary Killen

'A wonderful novel. Warm, sad, surprising and very, very funny. Barrow's ear for comic dialogue is genius.'
Daisy Waugh

'In *The Tap Dancer* Andrew Barrow has created, or perhaps more correctly re-created, a well-observed difficult father to take his place alongside other famously difficult fathers in fiction – variously shocking and monstrous, yet perceptive and endearing with his many recognisable foibles.'
Hugo Vickers

'Andrew Barrow's first novel is reminiscent of John Mortimer's *A Voyage Round My Father*. Both are portraits of ageing patriarchs whose behaviour is outrageously self-centred but who retain a place in their children's affections by their sheer eccentricity'
Sunday Telegraph

ANDREW BARROW

The Tap Dancer

HarperCollins*Publishers*

HarperCollins*Publishers*
1 London Bridge Street
London SE1 9GF
www.harpercollins.co.uk

HarperCollins*Publishers*
Macken House, 39/40 Mayor Street Upper
Dublin 1, D01 C8W8, Ireland

This paperback edition 2023
1

First published in 1992 by Gerald Duckworth & Co. Ltd 1992

A catalogue record for this book is
available from the British Library

ISBN 978-0-00-861917-6

Set in Sabon Lt Std by Palimpsest Book Production Ltd,
Falkirk, Stirlingshire

Printed and bound in the UK using
100% Renewable Energy at CPI Group (UK) Ltd

PART ONE

1

My mother and I watched the General Election results together. She was not at all politically minded but she breathed heavily during the announcement of Labour victories.

At one moment she tapped me on my arm with a banana and asked, 'Which seats were those? Do you remember?'

Finally, after we had watched the Prime Minister's triumphant arrival at his constituency, she said, 'I'm not really depressed by what's going to happen to our family but what will happen to the nation.'

My father wandered about the house smoking a cigar. He wore corduroy trousers, a flannel shirt sagging at the neck and a tweed jacket with a long slit up the back. He did not possess a single lightweight pair of trousers, a single lightweight shirt, pair of pants or pyjamas. Everything he wore was thick, heavy and kept in mothballs when he wasn't wearing it. A born pessimist, who always expected the worst to happen, he was not in the least upset by the Election results.

He wandered around the house much as on any other night.

'Hello, hello. This is clever,' he said to himself in a loud voice and then, 'Now, what are these things doing here?'

Again and again, my father went downstairs to turn off lights, lock doors, get a glass of beer, or check that I had not been downstairs and turned the lights on again. From my bedroom, I could hear his tread on the staircase, the change clinking in his pocket. Now he was pausing outside my door, breathing heavily through his nose. Now he was downstairs again, wrenching open an ill-fitting drawer and fumbling with an outer door. Soon I heard footsteps on the paving stones below my window.

A few minutes later, he entered my darkened bedroom.

'It's twenty-nine degrees outside. Three degrees of frost,' he said solemnly.

*

Life at home always remained on this level. Sometimes the big event of the week was the arrival of the dog's meat, held aloft by the pet shop man. The kitchen was the principal room; several generations of dogs lay there in different positions, sometimes hammering their tails against a chair or screwing up their eyes as they pressed against each others' sides. On the mantelpiece a cheap kitchen clock ticked extremely fast, while on the Aga a large kettle would hiss and rumble slowly up to boiling point. My mother would curse the vegetables she was trying to cook.

'Go on, potatoes. Boil!'

My father often sat nattering at the kitchen table, a crumpled newspaper in reading position on his lap. Sometimes he attempted to tap-dance on the cracked linoleum floor. Once he had slipped on something, looked down angrily to see what it was and couldn't help smiling when he found it was a banana skin.

At other times, my father withdrew to his study, sat in a low armchair permanently imprinted with his shape and read a railway guide. He was not usually planning to go anywhere but railways were one of his abiding interests. He turned the pages slowly and though he absorbed much of what was on them he could not prevent himself from also studying the hand that held the book. He clenched it, breathed heavily, then straightened it out like a flipper as if he was trying to read his own palm. Sooner or later, he would move over to the massive, old-fashioned filing cabinet. The prominent position which this occupied, its dilapidated state and bursting compartments reflected the amount of time and trouble my father took over family affairs. From time to time over the years I had opened it and found early drafts of his will, affectionate letters he and my mother had exchanged at the time of their engagement, files on each of his children, the house, the garden, and other aspects of domestic life. Many of his papers were jotted with extra thoughts – 'Points no longer applicable struck through' – and other explanatory notes.

*

We had lived in this house for about twelve years. It was a plain Victorian villa, eight miles out of Bath, onto which a bogus Georgian wing had been added, set in a sloping garden dotted with pine trees and evergreen shrubs in which wood pigeons occasionally sat hooting. My mother had done her best to create ordinary herbaceous borders and a large kitchen garden, but the pretentiousness of the original layout had proved impossible to eradicate.

Indoors, the house was an equally uneasy mixture of small rooms, narrow staircases lit by porthole windows, carpeted in a wide variety of different ways and filled with big mahogany furniture, much of which had passed through four or five generations of my father's family. The house was very uncomfortable. The heating system made a great deal of noise but provided little warmth. Beds wobbled and were mysteriously damp. Coat hangers rattled from hooks on the backs of doors. Clocks were unwound. Telephone mouthpieces were speckled with the food my father had spat into them. The house grated on my young sensibilities but my father seemed oblivious to things that would jar normal feelings. His bedside lamp was without a shade – he and my mother had occupied separate bedrooms for as long as I could remember – the hot water never came to his bathroom, and his medicine cabinet, crammed with sticky tubes of ointment, cod liver oil pills and other old-fashioned preventatives, hung off the wall at an odd angle. His bedroom was carpeted with a thick blue Wilton bought in a London house sale many years earlier, but his bed itself had two mattresses, which built it up to a disproportionate height, and beneath it sat a large chamber pot. My father was continually finding new ways to savage his surroundings – installing cheap fan-heaters, hanging up thermometers, replacing door handles, adding locks and bolts to windows and leaving sodden cigar ends in the bathroom basins. My mother may have objected to these defilements – and perhaps to the original purchase of the house – but her opinions carried little weight with my father and until recently she had had her hands full with more important work: the bringing up of five sons.

Now twenty years old, I was the last of this brood to be lingering at home. It is true that I had made a dramatic attempt to fly the nest the previous year by trying to enter the theatrical profession, but after thirteen months on the boards I had reluctantly returned home to 'think things over'.

The awkwardness of my position was emphasised by the fact that all my brothers had already settled down in their chosen careers. The eldest, Richard, married with two children, worked for a manufacturing company and lived in a small, smart house in West London. Tim, the second son, had started life as a picture restorer but at twenty-six had established himself as a painter in his own right. Easy-going but highly productive and with a sound commercial sense, he had spent most of this last year working in Italy – sending lots of postcards but otherwise keeping his distance. The middle son had fled far further. Fuzzy-haired and bespectacled, my brother Edward was now in the Far East working for an international bank, and was not due home on leave for another eighteen months. His current private life – particularly his involvement with native women – was the subject of jokey remarks by my father.

'Edward's grossly over-sexed, we all know that.'

My younger brother Ben, now eighteen and a half, had been a dunce at school – spending more than half his time in the bottom form and being constantly told to tidy up his appearance, though it was hardly his fault that most of his clothes had been handed down from brother to brother and by the time they reached him they were thoroughly worn out. This was a typical false economy on my parents' part: during Ben's last few terms at boarding school he had run up huge repair bills at the local tailors and immediately after leaving school had to enter a London hospital for an operation on his bunions caused by, the surgeon had no doubt, wearing ill-fitting shoes during his formative years.

All this was forgotten now. Ben had recently become uncannily well groomed and attired. The potato-faced adolescent had been transformed into a ripe peach. With just one 'O' level, however, he was considered good only for practical work. At the beginning of that year he had been enrolled at the hotel school in Vincent Square, Westminster, and was now learning elementary maths, how to make sauces, wait at table and carve a duck. The world of luxury he had entered contrasted as starkly with our home life as had the theatrical world into which I had attempted to jump.

*

My return home was an irritation to both my father and myself and there were a number of tense encounters in different parts of the house and garden.

'Yes, William?' he would ask whenever I appeared. Or, 'All right, William?' Or sometimes, 'Don't be a bloody fool, opening the gate like that!'

It was a relief when he went to London for the day – his brown and green garb replaced by a dark suit, stiff white collar, silver tie and the threads of his dark hair slicked back smartly. Until five years ago he had worked in London during the week – in the prosecutions department at the Board of Trade – and he had sometimes appeared at our boarding school quite dazzlingly dressed, a figure of almost Churchillian splendour, in pin-striped suit, gold watch chain, dark blue overcoat and bowler hat. He was far more at ease in London than in the country and his occasional day trips revitalised him.

He would go to the dentist, lunch at the Reform Club, where he had been a member since the end of the war, have his hair cut, see his stockbroker and return home on an evening train full of talk of changing times.

'You realise there's no bar at the Reform now? The members wanted waitress service and that was that.'

The journey itself delighted him. He had loved trains since

boyhood and during our own childhood had sometimes taken us to a local station just to see the Cornish Riviera Express hurtle through. He also loved meeting famous people on trains and rarely made a journey without some odd encounter.

'Sir Bernard Savoury was in the dining car,' he reported one evening. 'Complaining rather unnecessarily about the plates not being hot.'

My father's city clothes would then be folded away – with mothballs – and he would change back into an outsize flannel shirt, baggy tailor-made corduroys and a dirty camel-hair waist-coat which dangled over his crotch. His dapper London demeanour gave way to a prickliness and hostility to all that was soft and smooth. Instead of kissing or cuddling us, my father had sometimes grabbed us in a prickly bear hug from which I would clumsily recoil. He talked about sex as if it was some lavatorial function. Comments on masturbation, stainings and soilings were often on his lips. A phase of voluntary work on the local hospital board had added new terms to his already rich medical glossary. Phrases like 'anti-coagulants', 'post-operative distress', and 'nursing auxiliaries' were now part of his vocabulary and, along with the names of hospitals and asylums across the country, served to illustrate the strange medico-legal standpoint from which he looked at life.

My father loved his children but found fatherhood difficult. A flow of adverse comments fell from his lips, a mixture of harmless mockery and sombre discouragement which seemed designed to dismantle one's self-confidence.

'You've been to the commoner of the two big public schools', he said gloatingly.

No son was spared his abuse and even Richard was cut down to size. 'Richard's earning as much as a young dentist,' he said after his oldest son had been given a salary increase.

'Has Edward dined at the British Embassy yet?' he asked of his middle son.

This constant belittling and the frequently expressed prediction that most of his sons would end up in two-room council flats reflected his own timidity. Partly as a result of his work at the Board of Trade, he was pathologically law-abiding. The sinister phrase, 'known to the police', was one of his favourites, and several years earlier he had caused a minor sensation when he thought he had spotted the escaped convict Alfie Hinds on a railway train. On a humbler level, he had once picked up a sixpence in the road and then, fearing that he had been observed, had handed it to the village policeman. More recently, he had pointed out a pile of council gravel and said in his most menacing manner, 'If you picked up as little as a teaspoonful of that, you could be ruined for life!'

At other times he would launch into a blood-curdling imitation of a judge pronouncing sentence. 'North London games master . . . Heinous crime against those placed in your care . . . Ten years . . . penal . . . servitude!'

*

His most pessimistic pronouncements were reserved for me. He was now talking about the 'all-in lodging in Stepney', or 'cheap rooms in seedy parts of Hampstead' that I would have to endure if I tried to live in London without a job. He also tried to undermine me by constantly repeating that he did not think I would get married – but I had grown bored by this last line of attack and snapped back when he said it for the umpteenth time, 'So you've said. So you've said.'

It had not always been so. Many parents would have been horrified to learn that one of their children wanted to become a professional entertainer – but when shortly after leaving school I had declared this intention, my father had provided support and encouragement. Perhaps it was not so surprising. During his twenty-five years working in London, he had been a constant attender of music halls and throughout my childhood had talked about the acts that had delighted him. The names of Max Wall, Max Miller, Jewell and Warriss, Joan Rhodes, Diana Decker and other major and minor variety stars were often on his lips and, as I have said, he still tap-danced on the kitchen floor. It was he who had originally suggested that I contact the Bernard Delfont Agency and when at the beginning of the previous year I had gone north to Manchester to seek work as a stand-up comedian, he had entered into the spirit of the thing.

'Jolly good luck at the Custard House Hotel next week,' he had written to me after I had obtained my first professional booking. 'By the way, artistes do not drink with customers until after their last act. I hope your digs are fixed up.' A few weeks later, he had written, 'We hear you are still in Town and will not be on the Coast for the present,' and had scribbled a sketch of the London Palladium at the bottom of his letter.

Now that my theatrical career had been abandoned and I was back on home territory, my father had withdrawn into his other, inner self, lashing out nervously whenever we met in the house or grounds.

Even theatrical topics were taboo. One day that spring I had asked my father if a well-known actor who lived locally had been present at the golf club.

'No. And neither was Queenie Nancy.'

*

In spite of such bursts of hostility, my father thought about his sons constantly. He was always tinkering with our allowances, with his guarantees to our overdrafts, fussing over his gifts to us – recently we had each been given a roll of cloth which we had to use our own resources to have made up into a suit – playing us off against each other and worrying about each son in turn. At its worst, this took the form of will-dangling.

'Richard is my eldest son and therefore, quite naturally, gets slightly preferential treatment in my will,' was one line of attack. Another was, 'Sons who don't marry get less. That's perfectly obvious.' From time to time he tried to excite my interest in the mahogany furniture with which the house was filled.

'Richard gets nearly all the family furniture. He can look after it. I can't give furniture to sons who haven't got proper abodes. Why should I?'

This was strange talk from a man of only fifty-nine, who in spite of his hypochondria was in excellent health, but after several weeks at home I had grown immune to his outpourings.

I now saw that he lived in the past. He talked often of remote uncles, great-grandparents and cousins I had never met. The family had been Quaker since the early eighteenth century. My father was obsessed with his antecedents, with their clothes, money and appearance. During idle moments he sketched the design of their trouser turn-ups, and even the shape of their factory roofs, on the backs of envelopes and in the margins of newspapers. He had no illusions about them.

'Uncle Herbert wore a high round collar. He was a typical small manufacturer with all his capital in the works. He was worth about fifty thousand. His wife was worth about ten thousand, all in first-rate investments, of course . . . Great

Uncle Randolph looked and spoke like the minister of a large Baptist chapel . . .'

He made frequent comparisons between different antecedents and remote elderly cousins whom I had never met. 'Cousin Archie drinks a hell of a lot and smokes two cigars after every meal . . . Cousin Wilfred simply drinks, late at night, some strained lemon juice.'

His puritan background had made him something of a killjoy, self-obsessed and painfully money-minded. Wine bottles were corked up after two glasses had been poured, pleasures were programmed. 'We'll drink the rest of that after Doctor Finlay. It is excellent wine and we're not going to be immoderate about it.' He talked a lot about 'capital' and 'private money' and often expressed scorn for those who were not in business on their own. His talk was littered with counting-house expressions – 'private ledger', 'the cost of living index' – and the names of bank managers and other worthy figures occupied on the humbler levels of the financial world often came up in his conversations – Mr Trump, Mr Midwinter, Mr Sweet and Miss Moody. For Mr Sweet, who had been doing the family's accounts for the past twenty years, he had a special regard.

'Mr Sweet has visions of you in prison,' he remarked. 'You must pay your taxes.'

Sometimes my father's antiquated and cynical attitude towards life rang true.

'Nobody makes money from a job,' he said once. 'People do jobs because they haven't got any money.'

'Most people aren't particularly able,' he often said, and he had a particularly low opinion of his own abilities. 'From the age of seven,' he said, 'I knew I was not Prime Minister material.'

11

While claiming no superiority of any kind, he never admitted to being wrong. He never talked about the mysteries or beauties of life – 'Not bad, is it?' he replied when a visitor enthused over the sunset – and was infuriated by what he called 'grammar school, BBC-type responses'. Even his eldest son was accused of getting his knowledge of economics from newspapers and magazines. 'Richard takes what he reads in newspapers as gospel. He never reads basic books like *The Meaning of Money* by Hartley Withers.'

Poised uncomfortably between the upper and middle classes, my father was socially ambitious but didn't know what to do about it. By his own standards, he had made a good marriage. My mother's family had also been Quaker, but she was a descendant of various illustrious nineteenth-century bankers, brewers and philanthropists, whereas my father's forebears had been mill-owners, shop-keepers and chocolate manufacturers. When I was a small boy, my father had proudly shown me the entry for my mother's family in *Burke's Landed Gentry*. Unfortunately, my father's snobbery had closed many doors. It was beginning to dawn on me that, though he was often on the telephone and sometimes received a dozen letters a day, he had no real friends. Frightened of intimacy – he constantly warned me against 'inflamed friendships and provocative conversations' – he had taken refuge in such formalities and social rituals as still existed in the 1960s. He had developed over the years a set of fixed opinions on every minor and major matter, a rigid social creed and an unshakeable belief in How Life Should be Lived, which he was constantly trying to indoctrinate into his five sons by means of long monologues which he delivered with a ghastly expression on his face.

Instead of cultivating friendships within his own class, my

father had struck up acquaintances with people subservient to him. During his London phase he had got on wonderfully well with barmen, waiters, taxi drivers, policemen and commissionaires. Today, his main companions were the vicar, the village policeman, our part-time gardeners and the men at the local garage, where his large old-fashioned Rover was constantly being tinkered with. He talked at length to people outside the village post office and on street corners in the City of Bath, and extended formal invitations to some of these people to come and play on the three-hole golf course he had laid out in the garden. He was at ease with these acquaintances but kept his distance from them and was likely to sever the relationship if anyone started trying to call him by his first name – 'Christian-naming' was a subject on which he often talked with considerable anger. From these local worthies he was able to acquire a lot of gossip, and that winter had sometimes mocked my mother and me for our lack of knowledge of local affairs.

'But you don't seem to know anything about anybody . . . Colonel Cocky's war wound has started discharging again. Miss Fenton's got an incurable heart condition that could see her out in twelve to eighteen months . . . Half you people aren't on the bush telegraph at all.'

He was suspicious and dismissive of most of his neighbours and though initially sycophantic to local landowners and aristocrats he was just as likely to find fault with them if they were excessively friendly.

'Father now thinks Sir John is a sissy,' said my mother, explaining my father's new attitude to a local baronet who had invited them to lunch once too often that winter.

My father was hostile to homosexuals, foreigners, socialists, 'redbrick university cattle' and slickness of any sort. An elderly couple who lived on the edge of the village and happened to possess a cocktail trolly with seventy bottles of liqueurs in slots, were, he explained, 'Jewish and therefore quite naturally have all their goods in the shop window'. Another couple, equally showy in their own way, were he conceded 'not Jewish, but they have Jewish, St John's Wood ways'. A friendly airline pilot and his wife were described as having no background at all. 'Jack and Joan are Cockney people. Jack was, quite simply, a bright young chap in the RAF in peacetime, very likely not even commissioned.' A retired surveyor named Parker, who lived in the next village, was described as 'a mouldy old thing' and my father took a cynical view of another old neighbour's generosity as a host. Well of course, a man of that age is probably spending his capital.'

Alcoholics, too, were beyond the pale. 'Admiral Towpath is a tool house drinker,' he said of his nearest neighbour. 'Goes down to the end of the garden and drinks a bottle of gin in the greenhouse.'

*

My mother did not share my father's prejudices but made little attempt to check them. Her occasional interjection, 'Oh, do let me speak!' failed to halt the flow of his monologues. Though my mother spoke sentimentally about the early days of their engagement and marriage two years before the war – on the day of their engagement my father had given a London taxi driver his visiting card and said 'If there's ever anything I can do for you, let me know' – their relationship had long ago become badly disjointed. Not only did they have separate bedrooms, they also went on separate holidays. My father went off alone to play golf at Deal, Frinton or Carnoustie while my mother went back to her own mother, who lived on the edge of the Lake District, a woman whom my father had once feared and respected but now looked upon as rickety and tried to ridicule.

Recently, my father had begun to talk openly about the possibility of my mother dying and his subsequent re-marriage. One night that winter, he had said this loud and clear outside my mother's bedroom. He had then entered her room and remarked, 'Your lavatory's in a filthy state, dear,' and later I heard her murmur, 'You've got your teeth out, you old gaffer.'

My mother was admired by neighbours and relations for her serenity and patience; her slim figure had not been harmed by childbearing but she had acquired over the years the movements of an animal broken by drudgery. Tidying and mending had been her life. The house we occupied was the largest in the immediate neighbourhood, but my mother's reluctant attempts to play the role of Lady of the Manor had faltered on our first Christmas when she had taken some sprigs of holly to an old woman who lived in a nearby cottage. The woman had been overcome by embarrassment at the visit and had wet herself.

My mother was also shy, often hiding her face in her hands, blinking in photographs and unable to arch her neck or gaze confidently at anyone. She rarely wore make-up, usually forgot to use the expensive scent which her older sons sometimes gave her, and anyhow looked her best in cotton trousers or her old dark red velvet dressing-gown. She was most at ease, most tender, when dealing with flowers and animals. She kept hens and geese in a paddock adjoining the garden and that winter had looked after a broody goose during a blizzard. Coming in from the snow-covered garden one morning, she remarked, 'You've only got to see tracks in the snow to realise how purposefully people and animals walk.'

Now she was planting spring flowers. 'These little beggars were only put out yesterday. Healthy little plants,' she said approvingly. And re-potting another plant, she spoke to it as she did so, 'How pleased you must be to get into that.'

She was also devoted to her dogs, caring for them when they had worms – 'Tommy often toboggans along on his tail, which is usually a sign' – furious when the oldest and fattest dog Gilda came on heat – 'Wretched old woman, I could shake her!' – but was full of admiration for them when they did some brave deed.

For many years, the dogs had provided a further barrier between my parents. My mother cuddled, fondled and even reprimanded them instead of her spouse. My father was oblivious to these distractions, though he occasionally surprised everyone by making a remark about one of the dogs.

'Gilda is not at all well. Her head is wobbling in some sort of way.' In recent years, my mother had also developed a surprising passion for fishing. Now that her sons had grown up, she was free to visit rivers and reservoirs in the neighbourhood to fish for trout. She had even been to Scotland a few times – my father being on holiday elsewhere – and often spoke affectionately of the small hill loch where she had caught 'such millions of little tinies'.

Accompanying her on some of these local excursions, I had been struck by the fierceness of her manner, her angry glances at the water as she pursued her sport. At home, with an equally concentrated expression, she practised casting on the lawn, and in the back kitchen she sorted out satchels containing reels and flies. She said that her ambition was to catch a salmon.

*

My mother had only watched the General Election results that spring for sporting reasons, just as in due course she would watch the Grand National and probably the Derby. She had no real interest in the outside world. As a teenager she had been taken to Switzerland for skiing holidays and had once visited a missionary uncle in Palestine, but neither she nor my father had been abroad since their honeymoon in the South of France in February 1937. Now she declared that she would only go abroad to see the Oberammergau Passion Play. She was suspicious of what I had already decided were The Good Things In Life. She disliked London and was horrified by its traffic. 'I will not drive in London,' she had declared many years earlier. Her heart remained in Cumberland where she had been brought up and spent the first two years of her marriage and where her mother still lived. Signposts saying 'To the North' still thrilled her and she may have harboured some dim hope of eventually returning there.

Shy, sheltered and home-loving, my mother was a little disappointed by the careers her sons had chosen. Only for Tim's apparently happy-go-lucky life as a painter had she a certain sympathy and understanding. My own aspirations to go on the stage had been incomprehensible and during that traumatic spell of my life she had sent me somewhat disheartening letters.

'Thank you for your letter from Blackpool,' she had written in reply to a boastful and untruthful letter I had sent on hotel writing paper. 'Were you actually staying at the Imperial? Surely not the way to spend your precious money?'

Another time she had written, 'Father is rather annoyed by a bill from Moss Bros. for shirts, shoes and a camel-hair coat. I know I always ask you this but are you keeping accounts and do you put anything by for a rainy day? And do you ever go to church?'

Such critical questions had sometimes been followed by a rather deflating piece of domestic news. On the margin of one letter she had written 'The geese are laying, now and then, huge eggs.'

Even now, she would sometimes try to check my excesses, appointing herself the mouthpiece of the majority.

'William, you do make rather silly remarks sometimes,' or 'We don't want to hear, William,' were lines she could deliver with crushing authority.

Though she herself was not particularly philanthropic and had even once declared it would be fun to be a burglar, she had longed for at least one son to take up a career which involved caring for people or animals in an obvious way – to be a doctor, clergyman, farmer or vet. London bored her and she listened in a sullen manner to my father's warped observations on city life and occasional coarse jibes.

Many evenings ended with my mother sniffing and yawning – her yawns sounded like long musical notes – and eventually retiring to the back quarters of the house to prepare the dogs' supper. One night I found her here with a package in her hands.

'This parcel of meat has been dripping blood. How revolting of it,' she said.

*

A few days after the General Election, an event occurred which gave my mother a concrete reason for feeling low. The death at the age of eighty of her Aunt Amy, a comfortable spinster figure high up in the Girl Guide movement, was no great cause for sadness until after the funeral, when my mother was drawn aside by an embarrassed solicitor and informed that she and her five sons had been left out of the old lady's will.

All Aunt Amy's money had been given to more remote relations. My mother and her family were not even included
among those who were to receive small bequests, pieces of
jewellery and odd bits of furniture. Unmaterialistic though
she was, my mother felt humiliated by this surprising sting in
her aunt's tail.

'I felt very sad about it on the train. In fact I almost cried,'
she said after my father had collected her from the station.

'What does Father think?'

'Oh, Father's rather glum.'

When the news had sunk in properly, my father began to
react much more fiercely, at first directing his anger against
the main beneficiaries. 'That family don't get a penny out of
me,' he stormed. 'Your mother is terribly upset. I'd never do
a thing like Aunt Amy has done.'

He soon began new lines of speculation and attack. 'Was
she Socialist?' was followed by, 'Was she lesbian?' He then
tried to turn some of his anger on to me and my lack of
'capital'.

'You've only got five hundred pounds. It's pathetic! I had
ten thousand when I was your age.'

Aunt Amy's will was the principal subject for discussion
the following weekend when Richard and his wife Sally came
to stay.

'The important thing,' said Richard, 'is to try to find out
why she did it.'

Richard had changed. The tough little boy whose stern face
stared out of the family albums – the story went that on his
first day at prep school he had hit and knocked out a senior
boy – had been through various transformations since leaving
school. I remembered him in the army. I remembered him as
a dashing deb's delight, occasionally appearing at his old

school to take me out, his breath smelling of garlic, an early copy of *Private Eye* in the back of his car.

He had now emerged as a slightly harassed family man, who instead of teasing and bullying me, was avuncular, priding himself on his common sense but prone to a few throat-clearings and gruntings.

While Sally was bending over her younger child, my father pounced upon his oldest son and drew him into his study for a private talk, closing the door in my face. From the next room, I soon heard muffled voices. My father sounded excited, edgy, quarrelsome, extolling the basic principles of social conduct, illustrating his points with examples from his own early manhood, but constantly returning to the matter of the will. Twenty minutes later, Richard emerged and swaggered about the house, sighing importantly as he walked out of each room.

'What was Father talking about?' I asked.

'He talked about a lot of things he had on his mind,' he replied. 'Do you notice I'm looking frightfully fat?' he added, pulling up his jersey and flexing his stomach muscles.

The following morning, I helped him wash and polish his Volkswagen and in the afternoon he returned to London with his wife and children, leaving me to vegetate a little longer under my parents' roof.

My last few days at home were marked by the presence of my younger brother Ben, who was keen to exercise some of the new culinary skills he was now learning at the hotel school.

On the eve of my departure, he offered to cook a special meal. 'Oh, do persuade Ben not to mess up the meat,' begged my mother, 'It'll only make endless washing up,' but my brother stuck to his guns and prepared potatoes wrapped in oatmeal, cabbage in a cake and steaks in a delicious sauce.

My father did not like this food. His hand shot out for

mustard before he had tasted anything – and soon he was spitting out pieces of meat and giving them to the dogs.

Such were the circumstances in which I finally quit my father's house. Until the last moment, he remained obsessed by Aunt Amy's will, his fury now being concentrated on the fact that the document itself had been drawn up by one of the old lady's cousins, father of one of the chief beneficiaries.

'She ought to have been separately advised,' was his new war cry.

On my last morning in the house I found him penning a letter to his son in the Far East. 'The news about your Great Aunt's Will is indeed bad,' he wrote.

'Father can't forget it,' muttered my mother, too exhausted by the topic to feel bitter about it.

'Off you go, old boy!' said my father. Neither of my parents had asked me much about my plans, and as my mother drove me to the station, she merely murmured, 'It all sounds rather vague.'

2

I found a room in London and hung around the West End. I kept in touch with my parents by telephone but was sometimes dealt with rather summarily.

'I've got some bread in the oven and Tigger's squealing at the back door,' said my mother on one occasion.

'Where is it you're living?' she asked another time. 'A little basement place with its own bathroom?'

Soon after my departure I received a number of written communications from my father. A letter informing me that he had paid off my overdraft – 'You must now carry on on your own' – was followed by a terse postcard, 'I have asked the village shop to send you an account for certain purchases you made there in February and March. My mistake, no doubt, they were charged to me.'

A few weeks later, another letter from my father cautiously discussed the various career alternatives open to me. 'I am quite certain that something to do with the stage or screen – background or management – is more than likely to be your metier.'

On the margin of one of these letters my mother had added a piece of family news. 'Tim telephoned us last night from Rome. A complete surprise. We heard him very clearly.'

*

I also kept in touch with Richard – and paid various visits to his small end-of-terrace house on Campden Hill to discuss my Future. These appointments were preceded by a number of tricky telephone calls. The house was tiny but for some reason Richard and Sally took a long time to answer – and even when they eventually did so, I often heard a snatch of conversation before they actually said 'Hello'.

'Where are you?' said Richard with exaggerated excitement – or alarm – that I was in London. 'Lucky you didn't ring me two minutes later. You'd have found me in my bath. I much appreciate your ringing. Ring me again after the weekend. Look, we've got people coming at eight. That's fifteen, twenty minutes' time. When are you going home?'

Once when I had rung later in the evening he had exploded, 'What the hell do you mean by ringing at this hour? It's eleven o'clock! Sally's been asleep for an hour.'

'I didn't realise you went to bed so early,' I mumbled.

Another time I rang him at his office and he shouted down

the telephone, 'William, how are you?' as if he had not seen me for several years. Then in a quieter voice he added, 'Look, William, I'm in the middle of a meeting `. . .'

Eventually an invitation was extended – 'Come to supper on Sunday' – and I would make my way to Campden Hill.

The front door opened straight into the one cosy reception room, where the Sunday newspapers and their colour supplements would be neatly arranged on the padded chimney seat. On a side table stood framed photographs of their wedding four years earlier and on the walls hung paintings by my brother Tim.

'Let me take your coat,' said Richard stiffly. 'What can I get you to drink?'

He busied himself with a contraption for making tonic water and then said, 'Look, bring your drink upstairs.'

He led the way up the narrow staircase and I watched his grey flannel trousers twisting and curling, tightening and untightening, till we arrived at an attic room which was in some respects a replica of my father's study – with filing cabinet, ink bottles and blotting paper. It was not my first visit to this sanctum. Two years earlier I had been taken here to discuss my aspirations to be a professional comedian. Richard had been encouraging in his cautious way. He had warned me that I would meet a lot of sad people in show business – and he asked me if I had ever been to a showbiz party.

'Everybody calls each other darling,' he had informed me.

Today, he seized a clipboard and drew up a chart of various new careers open to me. We discussed the law – 'You've got to get into the right chambers' – and advertising – 'I think you can do better than that'. I said I would like to go to America but he dismissed this idea – 'You want to get more under your belt before you go to America.'

I said I would like to be a writer but he stifled this by saying, 'Could you write a pop song?'

Suddenly a cry from below interrupted us.

'Look, there's supper,' said Richard. 'We'll continue this afterwards.'

A tasty dish of barbecued ribs awaited us in the small, uncarpeted dining room. Sally was a radiant, domesticated woman, a Cordon Bleu cook, keen on yoghurt before it was widely available and a highly competent mother: both the children had been fast asleep for over an hour.

Conversation dragged during the meal. Richard mentioned that he had bought eighteen pairs of socks at Harrods the previous day. Sally played with the metal foil from the top of the wine bottle, squeezing it into various shapes while we talked about our parents.

'Your father seems to hate you,' Sally told me.

'The next fifteen years for Mother and Father are going to be very difficult,' said my brother.

We mentioned our brothers across the world. 'I would hate to work in Tokyo. It's a bastard city,' said Richard of Edward's current existence. Tim's easy life as a painter was more to his taste – 'I must say, Tim seems to lead a happy life, wherever he is' – but he seemed less convinced than I was of Ben's recent transformation. 'He's still pretty. stupid, isn't he?'

Then we washed up.

'It's amazing how much washing up even a simple meal can make,' Richard remarked and we then returned to the grim topic of my Future.

'My advice,' Richard said finally, 'is to get yourself an interim job. Even it it's only Harrods.'

*

Several such meetings occurred during the course of that summer. Sometimes Richard was bossy. 'Say thank you', 'Pass Sally the vegetables', 'Sit up' and 'Make sure it all goes in the ash tray.' If I ate too fast, he would say 'You must have been hungry', and if I overstayed my welcome, 'Don't stay any longer than you feel you want to.'

Sometimes he invited me to talk to him while he had his bath before dinner and I was obliged to watch his penis and scrotum swirling about in the soapy water.

Usually our meetings were threesomes – in which Sally played an increasingly small part – but one day a dapper army crony named Black was there when I arrived, trying to teach Richard how to play chess.

'Now you're in quite a strong position. You could move that piece up.'

'I'll bear it in mind but won't do it.'

'You're playing the caution game.'

'Unfortunately your bishop is precluding me from doing what I want to do.'

'You've got to take a risk sometime.'

Richard and Sally had a limited social life. Although, like many young couples, they occasionally attended some spectacular gala and earlier that summer had even been to a party that was also attended by the Rolling Stones, they did not participate on a regular basis in the new 'Swinging' London. Once, from the top of a bus, I had seen them shopping in King's Road, Chelsea. They seemed out of place. Richard looked ill, Sally uncomfortable in a bright red shiny mac. Instead they led an undramatic domestic life centred upon their two small children.

'Go and look at Sam on his baby bouncer,' said Richard when I called one afternoon.

We soon ceased to discuss my job hunting. 'How many refusals have you had?' asked Sally rather bluntly at the end of June. We turned to other subjects.

The topic of our parents was never far away and was tackled from a number of different angles.

'Father's got ten years of top golf before him,' said Richard one evening.

'Father married the wrong person,' he said another time. 'He should have married someone who kicked him up the pants a few times.'

Sometimes I talked about my life in London.

'How are you off for friends?' Richard asked suddenly.

'Are you lonely?' he asked another time.

*

My younger brother Ben and I also had our occasional meetings, though these were sometimes as tricky as those with Richard.

Our sessions in pubs were often marred by a certain fidget-iness on Ben's part.

'Drink up please,' he would say suddenly. 'I'm feeling very tired.' Sometimes I visited the hotel school itself. Each weekday, members of the public were welcomed to a cheap but formal lunch served by the students in a spacious dining room. Here I might find my brother in a long white apron pushing a sweet trolley with a self-mocking expression on his face.

'They say the students eat the mistakes in another room,' said a fellow customer.

From time to time I also visited Ben at the flat he shared with some other students, and occasionally I ran into him during my perambulations through the West End. One day I met him coming out of a launderette in Pimlico Road. Another time, I found him buying chef's knives in Old Compton Street.

Hard-working, practical and detached, Ben was learning to fend for himself. The previous year he had taken an amused interest in my showbiz aspirations, but he was now irritated by my idleness and twice that summer was to refuse to lend me money. This humiliating refusal created a gulf between us, and it was something of a relief when, at the end of the hotel school's summer term, he left London for six weeks' practical experience working in a motel in Canada.

*

At the end of the autumn I was offered a job as a trainee advertising copywriter – to start in the New Year – and with this small feather in my cap was able to confront my father again. Ben and I drove home together on the eve of my twenty-first birthday. A letter from my father prematurely congratulating me on this event had arrived at my lodgings three days earlier. He had added a postscript – 'A pair of gold cuff-links awaits you here' – but made no mention whatever of my new job.

As soon as we arrived at the house, my father made a bee-line for my younger brother and still did not mention the job. When I eventually raised the subject myself I was met with a torrent of anger. 'You've got to keep the job. You've got to get on with the people. You've got a job for a month, that's all. If they don't want you after a month, you'll get everybody's sympathy . . .'

Any praise over the matter was for my elder brother who had in fact played no part in it. 'Why did Richard select these people?' my father asked, and then turned on me again and started attacking the job itself, as usual putting it in the irrelevant context of his own early life.

'No. You've simply got a job that was paid the equivalent

of five pounds a week before the war. A clerk. That's all you are.'

He then added, 'I'm sure you'll earn your living with your pen,' which was more well-meaning but rather perverse considering that I had just been hired as a writer. This remark was to be echoed by the cleaning lady.

'I'm sure you'll prove yourself good,' she said. 'You'll get settled somewhere. You'll find your niche.'

Meanwhile my father taunted me about my birthday.

'Twenty-one tomorrow! Twenty-one tomorrow!' he chanted.

'It means nothing to me. I'd rather not celebrate it,' I said.

'Well, we're celebrating it!' he replied.

The house had not changed during my absence. Dogs dominated my mother's life, beds still wobbled when you climbed into them and new badly-placed handles caught your hand in the door frame as you moved from room to room. On my father's table there was a scattering of familiar correspondence. One was a letter from Tim, now painting in Philadelphia. There was also a letter from an old businessman who had recently been out East and met my brother Edward.

'I regard you both as fortunate parents. England needs as many young men of his type as she can get.'

The next day my birthday generated some genuine conviviality, though Ben remained detached from the proceedings and refused my father's offer of a cigar after dinner. Nor did the gold cuff-links materialise. Instead I was given fifteen pounds with which to make my own purchase. My father wrote out the cheque with an old fountain pen which worked like a matchstick dipped in ink.

3

I was not due to start the job till after Christmas and decided that I would spend most of this interlude at my grandmother's. She was my mother's mother – my only surviving grandparent and sister of the infamous Aunt Amy. She shared her life with my mother's unmarried older sister, Aunt Peg.

'I'm going up to Cumberland for a few weeks,' I told Richard.

'Oh, you are good,' he replied.

My grandmother lived in a spacious unheated house in a village on the edge of the fells. I arrived from the local station in driving rain. My grandmother and my aunt were waiting for me in the upstairs drawing room. Both hugged me.

My grandmother was eighty-eight years old, tall, formidable, with a big bumpy nose, almost blind but still able to plait her hair each morning and still running the household with an iron hand. Aunt Peg was fifty-seven, tall but ungainly, like a half-plucked hen. She was flamboyant and emotional, far more so than my mother, but her lips had a cruel blueness.

The house had a magic charm. There was a perpetual rush of wind along the upstairs passage, off which doors opened onto bedrooms which never changed. Pictures, ancient linen, smells and noises were exactly as they had always been. The staircase was hung with large framed photographs and engravings – including a picture of my bespectacled grandfather, who had died in the Great War leaving my grandmother to bring up her two little daughters alone. She had never remarried and still slept in the large high double-bed that she had shared with her husband. In her bedroom were some watercolours of Peg and my mother as children, in white cloaks and frilly bonnets with great bows under their chins. Peg looked tall, golden-haired and tempestuous. My mother was tiny and determined-looking.

Downstairs the house was equally agreeable, in the Beatrix Potter style, with scrubbed red sandstone floors, kitchen dresser, padded window seats and an elaborately chiming grandfather clock. The only untidy room in the house was my aunt's bedroom – which, in a gesture of independence and for easier access to the garden, she had chosen to have on the ground floor. The room was sometimes so crammed with rapidly discarded clothes that it was difficult to open the door. It was also icy cold as the window was kept permanently open to enable two cats to come and go as they pleased.

My grandmother still employed two people. One was Armstrong, whose pipe I had immediately smelt across the station on my arrival. A small, wiry handyman, who wore a beret and carried a number of knives stuck in his belt, he lived in a cottage which belonged to my grandmother across the village green. The other was Barbara Barton, a lumbering, snuffling Cumbrian woman, who slept at the end of the upstairs passage and who often joined us as we sat round the drawing-room fire.

It was here that spent most of the next few weeks, talking, reading, listening to the wireless – the News, The Archers, Any Questions chaired by Freddie Grisewood, and various concerts. Granny looked miserable and then fell asleep during Haydn's Clock Symphony but was always alert during The Archers or the News. Disasters shocked her. 'Poor things!' she muttered, but remained attentive for more details, and she was thoroughly diverted when, halfway through my visit, the Russian spy Blake was 'sprung' from a London prison. 'It was most awfully, wonderfully clever of them,' she repeated.

Most evenings I would read aloud to her from a newspaper,

but sometimes she would cut me off with, 'We won't read just now.' We also discussed topical issues. When my grandmother announced that she would like to have served on a jury, Aunt Peg said sharply, 'Oh Granny, did you want to hang somebody?'

My grandmother sat in a hideous modern chair: a recent acquisition which did not fit in with the comfortable old fireside furniture and was only justified because it was easy to get in and out of. Often she seemed to be fumbling for something, then pulled her skirt up over her knee – she had long slender legs – and removed a handkerchief from her knickers. Once a red hot twig flew out of the fire and landed on her lap. Barbara Barton lurched forward and brushed it away with a surprisingly deft movement.

Here we sat through stormy evenings, wind blowing down the chimney and shaking the windows.

'Do draw the curtains. I hate looking out at the black,' my grandmother would say while Aunt Peg read aloud from the *Daily Telegraph*, nervously scratching at the side of the newspaper as she did so and apparently oblivious to the weather howling outside.

Sometimes a cat joined the party.

'Here comes Catty,' said my grandmother, who had not attempted to grasp the distinction between the two animals.

Most evenings Peg and I played chess. My aunt was much keener on winning than I was and when I deliberated over my moves would hold a crooked finger to her lips, ready to pounce. Once her haste to make an offensive move was such that she sent a tin of toffees flying but she ignored this mishap and said 'Check' in a loud, sad voice.

After my grandmother and Barbara Barton had gone to bed, Peg and I would go on talking. My aunt and I were both 'outsiders' in our own ways. She had been something of a

secret support during my showbiz struggles the previous year
– though she claimed that she would never be able to come
and see me perform because theatre tickets were so expensive
and ventured one lethal piece of criticism: 'For a comedian,
you have a very ugly laugh.'

Nowadays, our conversations would usually centre on my
parents. These began mildly enough – 'Your father doesn't
think much of me' – but would often end with an outburst.

'Your father treats your mother like a slave!' screamed Aunt
Peg one evening.

*

We ate in the kitchen. My grandmother had given up cooking
– a mouse had been found in the soup. Barbara Barton had
taken over but served the same range of dishes. Mouse-free
but greasy soup, semolina, lentils and boiled brisket were
served without ceremony. 'That dish is red hot, Miss Peg,'
warned Barbara as she banged down a plate of meat – and
without alcoholic accompaniment. This Quakerish and
completely teetotal regime had been the subject of a certain
amount of criticism over the years from other members of the
family but had never mystified my father. 'Of course your
grandmother has no social life,' he had remarked several years
earlier, as if this explained everything.

This was not to say that my grandmother had lived as a
recluse. On the contrary she had been active in village and
country affairs and her life had been full of meetings. She had
been chairman of the Women's Land Army, vice-president of
the Women's Institute and on many other official bodies – and
she often spoke with affection of her former colleagues on
these committees.

'Sybil Hooker was always so forgetful but nobody minded

because she was so nice and good and easy,' she said of one old neighbour. Aunt Peg was still busy in these circles and had now been on the Cumberland County Council for almost twenty years. Over the years there had been many visitors to the house – including a black missionary who had attempted to enter Aunt Peg's bedroom during the night – but they were usually treated as social inferiors and sometimes given a patronising tour of the house.

'That's Elizabeth Fry,' said my grandmother as she passed a wax effigy on the half landing.

'Now what did she do?' enquired the visitor.

The tour proceeded to my grandmother's bedroom – and the portraits of Aunt Peg and my mother were pointed out. 'They were very attractive children,' said my grandmother.

Though her links with local society were now limited, my grandmother took a keen interest in her immediate neighbours. There was Miss Titty who had recently been removed to the local lunatic asylum – 'She threw her purse in the beck.' There was flashy Lady Somebody who occasionally appeared in the national newspapers – 'It is so terribly sad. I know she's a bad lot.' Then there was the vicar's wife who never attended the church – 'She doesn't fit into country life one bit.' My grandmother's oldest friend in the village was Mr Pickering, a retired solicitor who was now very ill.

My grandmother's house was in the middle of the village and had been the only house with a telephone, and as a child I had sometimes carried messages to nearby houses, entering a darkened parlour at five in the afternoon and finding a whole family sitting down to a big tea with lots of bread and butter beside their plates.

*

Many family holidays had been spent here. My father had usually stayed in a local hotel for a few days and then gone off somewhere else. His personality did not blend into this romantic lakeland setting and he had often spoken of how he would modernise the house, installing double-glazing, storage heaters, damp courses and other suburban defilements. 'I would close the back of the house and have your aunt's bedroom as a kitchen,' he had declared. 'And fancy a woman in your grandmother's financial position not having a double door!'

'The trouble with Cumberland,' he had thundered on another occasion, 'is that it has a bloody awful climate.'

My grandmother and my father disapproved of each other with equal gusto. 'Your father worries about himself, which is not very helpful,' said my grandmother that winter. 'He was badly brought up, spoiled, taken from school to school.'

My father's upbringing had certainly been strange. As an only child, whose own father had been killed in a London street accident shortly before the Great War, he had been brought up by his mother, a colourful but unstable figure – 'a little on the queer side' were Aunt Peg's words – who had cosseted him in various ways.

'Your father thinks too much about his money,' said my grandmother one night.

*

I had been at the house for about two weeks when Barbara Barton suddenly turned to me sharply at breakfast and asked, 'Did you know you were shouting in your sleep? At twenty past three I went along to your gran's room and you were shouting in your sleep.'

This revelation disturbed me, but during my waking hours I continued to prowl around the house, opening cupboards and drawers, seeking something to occupy my mind. In one desk I found a respectful letter to my grandmother from HM Inspector of Taxes. In another I found photograph albums from the early days of her marriage which included pictures of my grandfather fishing for salmon in his own river.

These investigations were not always happy ones. One afternoon I came across a letter that my sister-in-law Sally had written to my grandmother the previous winter. In a postscript, she had added, 'Rumour has it that William is not as keen on the stage as he was, which must please every member of the family.'

A few days later, I came upon a sad bundle of letters my grandmother had received after her husband's death in the trenches more than fifty years earlier.

*

For some time now my grandmother had made vague allusion to her own demise. 'I shan't be here then,' she said when certain future events were discussed. One night, after she had gone to bed, Aunt Peg explained that my grandmother looked upon her death as 'a trip to London – only she doesn't know when'.

Brought up to regard any tendency to question Christianity as a sin, my grandmother apparently assumed she would go straight to Heaven and be reunited with my grandfather.

'I'm not sure if Granny sees God as an old man with a beard,' said Peg, 'but she certainly believes that when you're in Heaven you'll have eyes, and ears, and arms, and legs!'

Every Sunday we would all walk the three hundred yards to church – my grandmother immaculately turned out and casting disapproving glances as Aunt Peg stumbled about the pews. After the service, conducted by a loud-spoken vicar, Peg hurried home crying, 'Ginger wine! Ginger wine!' as she entered the house.

Though a militant teetotaller, my aunt had been led to believe that ginger wine, of which she always looked forward to drinking a glass or two after church, was non-alcoholic. It was the openness that this drink produced in my aunt that caused her to declare one Sunday, 'The only reason for me living with Granny is because I'm her daughter.'

*

Whatever the dissimilarities between their characters, it was a complicated entanglement. When Peg went off one wet evening to a meeting in the village hall, my grandmother sat miserably at the drawing-room window.

'Yes, the hall is lit up now,' she said. 'I wish she'd come back. I didn't think she would have gone tonight.'

A few evenings later, I heard squabbling in my grandmother's bedroom.

'I'll just take your temp,' said my aunt.

'Oh, I don't think you need do that.'

'Oh yes I will, because if it's up at all you're not coming down to supper. It would be most unwise.'

A minute later, I heard my grandmother mumble, 'It's in as far as I can get it. I'm not cheating.'

A further argument took place over the thermometer's reading. 'The kitchen's just as warm as here,' my grandmother pleaded.

'Oh no it isn't.'

Suddenly my aunt became wildly emotional. 'I shall have

it on my conscience for ever if you come downstairs. I shall never be happy again.'

'I'm longing to go.'

'Look, yes, you're nearly choking now. But I'm the one who has to bear the burden for the rest of my life. That I killed you!'

My grandmother then stirred herself and said firmly, 'Really and truly, Peg, you mustn't let yourself get like this,' but nevertheless agreed to have supper in her bedroom and to take some cough mixture, which Armstrong was sent off to fetch the following morning. When Armstrong asked what size of bottle he should get, Barbara Barton perked up and said, 'I think there's just the one size.'

The following day an old doctor called and examined my grandmother.

'Could I just have a look at you? That'll do, yes.'

Later he said, 'I wonder if you'd take one of these small tablets every morning,' and closed his case with a thump and a click.

As he left the room, my grandmother asked about her old friend Mr Pickering.

'Oh, he's very ill.'

This answer did not satisfy my grandmother and I later heard her telephoning the vicar.

'Can you tell me about Mr Pickering?'

'Pardon?'

'Can you tell me about Mr Pickering?'

'Yes.'

'Has he gone to hospital?'

'He has,' the vicar intoned.

'Which one?'

'The Cottage Hospital.'

'What about Mrs Pickering?'

'She's staying here,' said the vicar, dismissing my grandmother as if she were a nuisance and a bore.

*

Towards the end of my stay Aunt Peg took me to a County Council meeting in a field. A man in green knickerbockers and a deerstalker hat, worn on top of scruffy schoolmaster's curls, took charge. My aunt stumbled about with her hands on her hips.

Armstrong and I watched the meeting from the well-kept Morris Minor, with which my grandmother had replaced the Vauxhalls and Daimlers of the past.

'They're not all clever,' said Armstrong. 'They're just in the position to do it.'

'I'm finished now,' said Aunt Peg, suddenly back at the car.

*

Under Barbara Barton's care, my grandmother's health improved but she continued to worry about her friend Mr Pickering.

'Yes?' said the vicar when she telephoned him for the third or fourth time.

'What is the news about Mr Pickering?'

'It's sad, I'm afraid.'

'Oh dear.'

'He died last evening at eight o'clock,' said the vicar in his sing-song voice.

*

Life sailed on – as it would after I had left. Armstrong came in and out each day with fuel for the Aga and the drawing-room fire, his beret on the back of his head and a cheery 'Righto, Miss Peg' for my aunt. One morning he told me he had sat up all night with his family watching the Royal Variety Show. Every morning, Aunt Peg shouted on the downstairs telephone about County Council matters and then battered on the lavatory door when I was inside. The two cats threaded themselves through the banisters.

'At a quarter to seven I put the tin hot water bottle in your gran's bed,' said Barbara Barton, explaining her own routines. 'Then at nine, or half past nine, I put in the rubber one with a nightie round it so it's nice and warm when she gets in.'

4

I returned to my father's house for Christmas but was there for just a few days before starting the job in London. Henceforth I would make only brief visits to my parents and would watch their ups and downs from the half-detached viewpoint of a weekend guest.

Usually I went by train, bracing myself in the crowded carriage for the onslaught ahead. Once, there was no seat at all and I travelled home in the goods van with a crate of Camembert and some midget Red Cheshire cheeses bound for Tintagel. My visits were negotiated in advance and were sometimes even the subject of letters from my father.

'If you take a bus or taxi from the station on Friday night,' he wrote on one occasion, 'I will drive you to the station on Sunday night. Very glad to hear that your work, so far, is going well.'

My mother and father never came to meet me together. Sometimes I would find my mother waiting quietly in the car. At other times my father was making his presence felt at the station newsagent. He cut an odd figure in his check cap, camel hair waistcoat and Tootal tie, mixing momentarily with less formally dressed neighbours who were also meeting weekend guests.

Sometimes I took a taxi from the station and arrived at the house in the small hours. I would then enter by the back door and pass through a room containing brushes, mops, pulleys, a butler's tray, wastepaper sacks and my mother's fishing tackle.

In the kitchen, I would find the dogs in a heap beside the Aga, oblivious to the mice on the work tops and the silverfish wriggling across the floor. Sometimes there was a note in my father's handwriting – 'Do not have a bath tonight' – and in the morning he would praise me for my stealthiness.

'I do congratulate you on the way you came in last night. An example to everybody.'

Sometimes Richard and Sally or Ben had got there before me. The empty claret bottle and two cigar ends in the kitchen waste-bin revealed that my father and one of his sons had already had their first session, and I might later hear a sibling's footstep in the second bathroom.

One weekend, Richard arrived a few minutes after I had been collected from the station and I heard his feet on the metal doormat at the front door.

'When did you arrive?' he asked in a not entirely friendly manner, but later he cornered me and asked in a rather excited voice about my new job.

'Have you written your first ad?'

He continued on this lively note for most of the weekend,

eventually declaring, 'You could be writing the best copy in the agency within a month.'

My father's mood was also unpredictable. Sometimes his lips seemed to curl when I entered the room, but often he would relax a little and tease me about my work.

'Have you had any official reprimand yet?'

The good humour never lasted for long, however, and sooner or later sparks flew in different directions.

'I think Sally has misunderstood what I said,' muttered my father one morning.

'I wasn't listening,' snapped his daughter-in-law.

'What's the joke, William?' said Richard, when I smiled at his new check cap and tweed jacket.

*

One weekend, violence broke out immediately over my new hair-cut – or was it the smell of the hairdressing?

'How can you expect provision to be made for you in wills if you behave like that?' said my father. 'Don't model yourself on clerks – that's all you are at the moment!'

'I'm not working for the Board of Trade,' I replied, my blood boiling. 'I don't care where you're working. We couldn't invite anyone at all here to meet you.'

He flexed his newspaper like a weapon and muttered, 'You come here smelling like a borstal boy.'

'You're going to be bald soon, anyway,' said my mother.

Neither of my parents were able to understand what copy-writing was.

'What is this work?' asked my mother. 'You're given things to fill in?'

'Anyhow, you're only on probation,' said my father.

That night he entered my bedroom and spoke more mildly

41

about office life – 'Does the tea come to you or do you go to the tea?' – and asked me how I spent my lunch hours.

'What you want is a proper public house roast,' he insisted.

The next morning, he reverted to the same old line of attack.

'Of course you're a clerk. What training have you had? What qualifications have you got?'

My brother Ben somehow escaped all this. Tidy, self-possessed and sticking to his studies at the hotel school, he drew few rebukes from my father.

'In Father's eyes,' said my mother, 'Ben can do no harm. I stick up for you until I'm blue in the face.'

*

Most weekends there were little changes to discover, more security devices or unnecessary decorative additions. The new Persian rugs on the landing would, my father explained, eventually go into 'the cottages or cow houses my sons live in', and he had plans afoot to re-upholster the armchairs in the drawing room and fit brass castors to their feet.

This new passion for having everything on castors made the house even odder. Beds now leapt from the wall as you climbed into them and armchairs shot back across the room when you sat in them. One weekend I found my father talking to the upholsterer on the telephone and planning further innovations.

'Does it matter if the tassels touch those revolving balls? There's no danger of them getting muddled up, is there? Surely there must be a clearance? For the red chair, simply the braid. Eleven yards will do the whole thing.'

My father would also fill us in on any new events or activities in the neighbourhood.

'Colonel Cocky's been in most frightfully low water since

you were last here . . . Had dinner with Daintrey last night. Wish his wife would learn to cook . . . Mrs Smith's had her baby. All done on the State, of course.'

'Of course,' said Richard.

Sooner or later my father would drag away his eldest son for a private talk. Within seconds of the study door closing I heard my father's artificial cough. Soon they were talking about golf clubs.

'D'you reckon I ought to buy a better set?' asked Richard.

'Have you played with your managing director yet?'

'I am on Tuesday.'

'You'll let him win, of course.'

'When are you coming to London?'

'I've been.'

Banalities of this nature were soon dispensed with and my father cleared his throat again and said, 'Well now, Richard, what is the position with . . .' and would launch into a monologue on his current obsession. 'How long do you think William will stay with these people?'

To this and other wranglings my brother would listen cautiously, allowing himself only a few grunts and throat clearings.

We were all occasionally subjected to these solo sessions – and each reacted in his different way. Ben usually sailed through them with humorous detachment, but Richard would emerge strung up by the ordeal. Sometimes he sighed, 'I try to say what I can to help. Got a cigarette? No? Dammit!'

Then his ill spirits got the better of him. 'Would you like to take the wireless next door because I've now got to use the telephone.'

Slowly the day wound down and one found oneself eating supper off a trolley in front of the television.

43

'Oh, isn't he revolting?' said my mother when a bearded jazz musician appeared on the screen. 'Go away!'

'Who are these?' said my father entering the room. 'Are these the Beatles?'

He sat down for a second but was soon declaring, 'This is a whole lot of working-class rubbish straight out of the gutter!'

He perked up a bit when a comedian came on but instead of laughing at the jokes said thoughtfully, 'That's quite a well-cut suit, you know.'

'Get up,' said my mother eventually, 'I can't get out with the trolley.'

'Mamma, you look so tired,' said Sally.

'Let's all go to bed,' said my mother, but she made no attempt to move for several minutes and an hour later her bedroom light was still on.

The evening ended with my father trying to hurry us off and failing to do so, repeatedly reminding us to turn off the gas fire and unplug the television.

'He can't help it,' whispered Ben. 'It's a disease.'

My father then reappeared and said solemnly, 'I'm going to church tomorrow. The vicar is preaching.'

He appeared again while I was getting undressed.

'Can you sell me a cigarette?' he asked.

*

Mornings followed a similar pattern. My mother had a fear of stale cereals and her first task of the day was to take the cornflakes out of their packet, re-heat them in the oven and then place them in a plastic bag secured with a clothes peg. Breakfast was served in two or three sittings.

'Shall we clear this debris away before the others come down?' asked my mother.

My father was the last to arrive – and was often in a temper, sometimes throwing the newspapers out of the room and declaring that he wanted to 'communicate' with me or, on other occasions, hurling abuse.

'You haven't brushed your hair this morning, old chap. You look half cracked.'

Breakfast ended with Richard whistling loudly as he cleared away with the aid of a semi-circular brush and crumb-board.

On Sundays, the church service loomed ahead. In spite of his Quaker upbringing, my father had always preferred the Anglican form of worship and had to a large extent turned against Quakerism, which he now considered attracted mainly socialists and university professors. He also had a high regard for the local vicar's political standpoint.

'Our vicar is not a Labour vicar. Not a Labour vicar,' he repeated.

On Saturday morning, my father would retire to open his letters. One weekend these included a letter from Tim, which contained the statesman-like sentence, 'I was concerned to hear of fighting in Jordan.' Another weekend my father tore open a big envelope from the Lord Chamberlain's Office and remarked, 'Now this is a pleasant thing.'

Inside was an invitation to a garden party at Buckingham Palace, an acknowledgment of his five years' service on the local hospital board.

5

'It faces north, doesn't it? You'll be sitting there all day with the light on,' said Richard.

At the beginning of that spring I had decided, against everyone's advice, to lease a small unfurnished flat in a dingy street near South Kensington station. Richard's observation was true enough, but when I remembered that his own house faced north, I decided to ignore his argument.

My mother had sent a postcard pleading with me to consider a less expensive area. She had quoted an example of some distant double-barrelled cousins who lived in Battersea. 'It does seem foolish,' she wrote, 'to start with a good address and then perhaps move down.'

My father had at first been mildly in favour of the plan – 'Can you cook yourself a meal?' – but was soon threatening to withhold furniture and other chattels until he had scrutinised the lease and, in the last few days before I finally committed myself, had repeatedly telephoned my lodgings.

On these occasions my mother acted as 'operator'. She was always the first to speak, establishing my availability. Then my father came on the line and uttered, after a moment's hesitation, a pre-prepared speech of considerable ferocity.

'Oh yes-er-now-nothing-leaves-this-house-until-I-have-given-my-seal-of-approval-to-the-lease.'

A few more words like this and my mother would come back on the line and speak more mildly.

'I don't think you can really expect much from here. Father definitely wants to let the back of the house next year.'

In the event, I signed the lease and my father provided me with certain basic furnishings and advice.

'A good second-hand three-foot mattress can be bought for about eight pounds,' he wrote. 'A three-foot bedstead is here for you.'

As so often, he then seemed to change his tune completely,

telephoning me at my new home saying, 'There's lots more for you to collect here.'

*

My acquisition of the flat was followed by a further undertaking. With some apprehension on both sides, it was agreed that my younger brother should share the place with me. My job in advertising had re-established me in Ben's good books. He was still at the hotel school and it seemed possible that we would see little of each other. His catering skills were welcome in a flatmate and he was domesticated in other ways, having learnt how to sew on buttons and iron shirts as well as prepare beautiful-looking food.

Thus it was that Ben moved into the flat, along with his chef's knives, heavy chopping board and two large suitcases containing most of his wordly goods.

Ben's character remained unfathomable. He was superficially the most debonair of my brothers, his hair was always tidy and his repartee was remarkably clipped for a twenty-year-old, but underneath this façade he was an unknown quantity.

Our life fell at once into a routine. Ben was a creature of habit. He had two alarm clocks, which rang loud enough to wake up the neighbours. He was always up before me and would enter my room before leaving for the school with a staccato, 'Mornin', seven-thirty.' On the evenings when he was not occupied elsewhere he would busy himself in the kitchen, preparing supper, sniffing as he did so, the squeak of his shoes on the lino interspersed with the smack of the fridge door closing, a trickle of water or the whirr of a hand-operated food whisk. He did all these tasks in the way he had been trained, with a deadly calm, and I was surprised one night to hear a piece of crockery smashing.

'Hello. What went?' I asked, after a pause.

'Mug,' he said, after another pause.

Later, we might relax a little over some fancy dish he had prepared and talk companionably about the family from which we had sprung.

'We've had a very hard time with Father,' said Ben one evening. 'He's given us a lot of trouble.'

Sometimes our conversations would develop into imaginative speculations.

'Supposing,' Ben suggested one evening, 'Father hadn't had his hair cut since leaving the Board of Trade?'

Sooner or later, my younger brother would return to the kitchen and I would hear the hiss of aerosol starch followed by the thump of an iron. Then he would clean his shoes for the next day and put on the kettle for his hot-water bottle, a habit which seemed to have stuck with him since childhood.

Finally, he would appear in the doorway of my room, give me a stagey grin and say 'G'night', before retiring to his own room a few feet away, where I would soon hear him winding his alarm clocks, often accidentally activating one or both in the process.

6

Summer came. Ben and I went home together in his grey van. There were fresh laurel trimmings on the drive and round the corner we found my father brandishing his new Wilkinson Sword shears.

He made a movement to get us into the house, and once inside to push us from one room to another.

'You're in the end room. Ben's next to me,' said my mother. 'Get into some summer clothes and help Richard with the tennis netting,' she ordered.

Our eldest brother was already there, in gym shoes and no socks, his jersey pulled up at the sleeves, a mug of tea in one hand and an ashtray in the other. Apparently there had been a scene between Sally and my father the previous weekend and she had decided to remain in London with the children.

'I'm afraid I lost my temper with Sally,' my father said solemnly.

'They were snapping at each other all the time,' said my mother. 'Father's looked rather grim about it all week.'

This family squabble coincided with the Six Day War, and that evening I found my mother hunched in front of the television with her most serious expression on her face.

'You'll all be called up,' she said grimly.

The following day, my mother pulled herself together and prepared a picnic lunch in the garden.

'I wish I could sit down without being covered in dogs,' said my mother. 'Yes, I know it's a hot day, Gilda.'

'Go away, wasp!' she said a few minutes later.

'Ooooh! It's a queen wasp!' exclaimed my father, a reluctant participant in these outdoor meals. 'A huge animal!'

The following week, my parents would go to the garden party at Buckingham Palace.

'Will you have to curtsey?' the cleaning lady asked my mother. 'I suppose you'll have to go down like this – I can't go down because my knees are too cronky.'

My father responded to this attempted demonstration by

saying, 'God Almighty!' but in fact he was looking forward to the event.

'The Queen Mother really stole the show,' he said the following weekend. 'The Queen is a small slight woman, unapproachable.'

He continued to ponder over the event.

'Those men in morning coats who tell you rather sharply to get in line would be very foxed if you didn't bunch.'

*

Occasionally my visits home coincided with those of others. The sound of a cautiously driven vehicle on the gravel often indicated the arrival for tea of some hospital board colleague of my father or of some minor dignitary currently under my father's patronage. There were also overnight visits from cousins, old friends of my mother's, and, one weekend, from a rather glamorous spinster called Bobbie who had vaguely figured throughout my childhood.

'She was my girl-friend,' said my father in a solemn voice as the little shooting-brake drew up at the front door.

The car door opened and there was a puff of scent. Bobbie noted the mileage and then got out. She had dyed blonde hair and wore pink trousers. She did some stretch exercises before greeting my parents and winking at me.

She carried a bottle of vodka which she immediately placed in a niche in the dining-room skirting board, a silver cigarette holder and a packet of Three Castles, which she described as 'an old-fashioned fag'.

For the next thirty-six hours, Bobbie trotted about the house, supervising and commenting on the arrangements. She interfered with the cooking – 'Making scrambled egg is like mowing the lawn. If you poke at it too much it just gets into a straggly mess' – and wiggled her body between my mother and the kettle in order to fill her hot-water bottle, which was contained in a fancy but threadbare velvet cover.

She offered me her vodka, quizzed me about my theatrical experiences – 'You must have met some deliciously crumby people'; spoke disparagingly about my current job as an advertising copywriter – 'I should think you could do that without the slightest difficulty'; and made rude comments about my parents' marriage – 'Your mother did her best with poor material.'

Finally, on the doorstep, she said in front of everyone, 'I decided pretty early on that your father was not for me.'

'That's a nasty one,' I murmured.

'I thought so too,' said my mother. 'That's why I'm going to turn my back on her.'

'A very tiring woman, Bobbie,' said my father after the annual visit was over.

*

I never lingered beyond the weekend – but always found departure difficult. My father pushed me away with his gruff, 'Off you go, old boy,' but my mother sometimes pleaded with Ben and me to stay: 'Seems a horrid night for going back. Sure you wouldn't like to leave in the morning?'

Richard also made heavy weather of departure, announcing pompously, 'The car is now loaded. Which has exhausted me.'

Often my mother would hold herself back: 'I won't kiss you because I've got a cold coming on.'

My father had now ceased to make comments on the lowliness of my job but had found a new line of attack.

'You're very shy. That's your trouble. You're very shy. You

want to meet more people,' he said as he drove me to the station one Sunday night. 'I've asked Richard to get you on to a hostess's list.'

7

Like my father, I had almost no friends. Till now my social life had been limited to outings to local restaurants with Ben, meals with Richard, and the occasional visits that colleagues from the advertising agency cared to pay me.

These excursions with Ben were not easy occasions. Superficially smooth, Ben was all elbows when we were squeezed together in a cheap restaurant, and his shrewd or sarcastic comments on the food we ate – 'Cook's got a headache', 'Parsley is only to make food look pretty', 'A cup of coffee costs them a farthing' – introduced another element of spikiness.

Among colleagues who visited me was a skinny ginger-haired copywriter named Peter Cooper. He was an American, a would-be author some four years my senior – and a possible source of useful advice. On one of his first visits I had shown him my early attempts at a novel. With a glass of wine balanced on the arm of his chair, he had begun reading my scrappy manuscript.

'Jesus!' he said after a few moments, 'It's really fantastic. This'll win you thousands of readers, plus sales. Jesus, it's really interesting.'

He scratched his head excitedly, then his armpit. Then he gave a yawn.

'Oh shit!' he said. 'Not so good. Terribly boring. Oh, Jesus, it's bloody boring!'

Despite these mixed reactions to my writing, Peter became

a companion to both Ben and me, joined us on some of our excursions and occasionally made perceptive remarks about us.

'Ben looks as though he's going to explode,' he said of my younger brother.

'You're all nerves anywhere outside your apartment,' he said of me.

Occasionally, Ben introduced me to his acquaintances in the catering trade. One breezy young man called Len owned a wine bar. The discovery of this man's existence in his youngest son's life had caused a ferocious momentary eruption from my father – 'I know those busy little men,' he had snarled. 'They do you ten little good turns and then one bloody big bad turn' – but as so often with my father the matter had soon been forgotten or dislodged by some other crisis or obsession. Len still sometimes invited Ben to supper and seemed to encourage in my younger brother a sort of fawning obedience.

*

Now Ben and I began to receive more agreeable invitations and during the autumn were invited to a few seasonal cocktail parties. Ben dismissed these events as 'thoroughly low-powered and pathetic' and the people there as 'a load of duds', but he accepted the invitations all the same. 'Short of single men,' he explained.

As far as I knew Richard had played no part in this turn of events, but he now urged us to expand our circle much further.

'I want you both to get five names and addresses at each party you go to,' he said aggressively. 'Even if they look like the back end of a bus.'

It was on one of these occasions that Ben met Mary York. She looked like Alice in Wonderland and had her own quaint style of dress – red velvet knickerbockers, big white bows and a white powdered face. She seemed to hang on Ben's every word, but it was soon clear that he was not interested in discussing the relationship.

'How's Mary?' I asked.

'Fine,' he snapped.

When I tried to press the matter he responded crossly, 'I've already said she's fine. Please don't ask me the same question again.'

The relationship appeared to flourish, however, and would have been greeted with considerable interest by my father had not his attention suddenly been turned to another matter altogether.

8

My brother Edward – enigmatic, tight-lipped Edward – had avoided my father's censure for the last two years by living abroad. The file that my father kept on his third son had little in it. Austere, typewritten letters, sometimes signed off 'Kind personal regards', arrived often from the Far East but they never gave my father anything to worry about.

In December 1967 all this changed and all other family problems, real or imagined, were thrown into relief when a short handwritten letter arrived from Edward announcing that he was to marry a Japanese girl.

'Father just roared with laughter,' said my mother the first weekend after this bombshell.

The laughter had quickly died away and my father was now very worked up indeed. While my mother made soft pecking noises in the long flowerless border outside his study window, abuse and anger poured from his lips in a torrent of ferocity.

'Our marriage has gone well. Until now. There was bound to be one of you who was going to be a bloody fool. I'll tell you this – there's no great joy in Colonel Cocky's house about this matter.'

Ben and I had received the news with some amazement, but as so often before my younger brother kept his own counsel – and anyhow now had a problem of his own. For the third time running, he had failed an elementary maths test at the hotel school, and though his other work there was quite adequate, he had been told he must leave at once. 'It makes no difference at all whether I am at the hotel school or not,' he said stubbornly, yet begged his brothers not to disclose what had occurred. My father was thus spared this diversion and could concentrate his full attention on Edward's marriage plans.

The slim file that my father kept on his third son had suddenly expanded dramatically. I soon opened it and found handwritten copies of letters my father had addressed not only to Edward, but also to the managing director of the bank for which he worked, to the family solicitor and even to the British Ambassador in Japan.

The same phrases appeared in each letter: '. . . This difficult situation. I just cannot see such a marriage being other than an exceedingly unhappy one . . . divorce and separation rates for mixed marriages are, I am told, high . . .'

His grimmest words were reserved for the Japanese themselves: '. . . These people,' he scribbled in a postscript to one letter, 'who so rightly received a dose of their own medicine in the summer of 1945.'

There were also a number of international calls – my

mother's excited smile on hearing her son's voice counterbalanced by my father's anxiety about the telephone bill – and the arrival of further letters from Edward along with coloured photographs of Michiko – pert, tiny and dressed in a kimono – did little to soothe things. In a letter to me, Edward described our father's reactions as 'understandable and inevitable' but made it clear that his mind was set.

After a few weeks my father seemed to have come to terms with the situation and referred to it in a lighter vein. When a date for the nuptials was announced, he told various acquaintances, 'My third son makes a bloody fool of himself on the 27th.' In a jokey letter to me my father wrote, 'I am recommending Edward to have a second look at Quakerism. He could fit in most happily. A tolerant little community who are most likely to accept mixed marriages and their offspring.

My mother kept her feelings to herself, but wrote a friendly letter to her prospective daughter-in-law, welcoming her into the family and expressing her longing to see them both when they came to England the following year.

In due course the marriage took place in Tokyo. No one from the bridegroom's family was present; but we were sent photographs of the wedding banquet at which my kimono-clad brother sat beside his bride looking as inscrutable as ever.

Suddenly the whole thing had become a joke again – 'What news of the foolish son?' – and my father made no attempt to master his new daughter-in-law's name.

One Saturday morning, I found him leaning forward over the breakfast table and scratching at something with a knife. His eyes lit up mischievously.

'Look,' he said, 'I've done Koko in the butter.'

9

Ben settled happily in the kitchens of the Dorchester Hotel. He had got the job within a few days of his ejection from the hotel school – and was once again the blue-eyed boy.

My father's mind soon began to focus on other problems. The chief of these was the running cost of the house. From time to time he would mention the possibility of letting the back of the house – or some other more drastic arrangement.

'Oh, he does vaguely talk about it when he gets depressed here, just us alone,' said my mother. 'A flat in London and a cottage in Wiltshire. I have no desire to live in London . . .'

Suddenly it occurred to my father that another temporary solution could be achieved if his mother-in-law could be persuaded to come and live with us as a paying guest. Rapidly, a plan formed that my grandmother, now eighty-nine years old and steadily failing, should sell her house and come and live with my parents in Wiltshire. Aunt Peg would fulfil a lifetime's ambition by moving to a cottage of her own in Cumberland. My mother was said to welcome the proposal. She adored her mother and was glad to let Aunt Peg acquire a home of her own at last.

The plan was drawn up carefully. A folder marked with my grandmother's initials was added to the bursting filing cabinet and in it I found a copy of a carefully worded letter my father had sent to the old lady's lawyers proposing that she should pay so much a quarter during her stay. 'On our part,' he had written, 'we would supply all bedding, furniture and food, a glass of sherry when she wants one, full use of the garden and drives in my car. We shall be very happy to have Granny here, will do all we can to make her happy and introduce her to the few very old people living here whom we think she would like – about four of them. Lastly,' he had added, 'if the cost of living index is allowed to rise rapidly, I would give you at least six months' notice of any proposed raising of the quarterly payment.'

These negotiations coincided with the advertising of my grandmother's house and Aunt Peg's selection of a tumbledown cottage a few miles away. The whole upheaval – and in particular the clipping of my grandmother's wings – represented a sort of triumph for my father. The formidable woman he once feared, respected and sucked up to, was now under his thumb – and would pay heavily for the privilege.

*

In the spring of 1968 my grandmother arrived in Wiltshire. She brought with her a silver-topped cane, two wirelesses, a Talking Book For the Use of the Blind, her large high double bed, her nasty modern chair, and – most important as we had hitherto been a one-car family – her well-serviced Morris Minor.

She also brought Barbara Barton. Armstrong had decided to seek another job in Cumberland, but Barbara reckoned that her place was at my grandmother's side. It had been arranged that she would occupy a bedroom at the back of the house which had once been Edward's.

As soon as my grandmother arrived, my father began to mock and taunt her.

'Now then, Granny. All right?' he asked when he ran into her hobbling along a passage.

'Yes, thank you,' she said.

'Got your collection money, Granny?' he asked as we set off for church the first Sunday after her arrival.

'Glass of whisky, old boy?' he offered me after dinner. He had never suggested this before and was doing it to try to annoy his mother-in-law, whom he still thought of as prim and school-mistressy – 'Granny looks upon the Dorchester Hotel as the haunt of sin' – and he had already shown me the specially small wine glass he had selected for her sherry.

Granny seemed largely immune to this teasing. Perhaps she was too blind and deaf to know what was going on, though she still plaited her hair neatly every morning and was a figure of some dignity. She sometimes craned her neck to stare at me in a bewildered manner, but she often looked alert and amused, her old eyes still sparkled and her face lit up with great charm.

'You've got nice lodgings in London?' she asked me amiably and then talked about Aunt Peg's new home. 'Oh, it's a very good little house, it'll do Peg very well.'

Your grandmother's so regal,' said Sally, whose weekend visits had now been resumed.

Inevitably, there were a few difficulties to start with. The dogs were disturbed by my grandmother's presence and barked at the sound of her Talking Book.

'All right, all right. Don't you bark, dogs,' said Granny, her long legs accidentally kicking one of the dogs away from the fire. The dog sniffed at the foot that had kicked it and then alarmed the old lady by leaping on to her lap.

The layout of the house was not suitable for an old person. 'Granny doesn't like having stairs to contend with,' commented my father as his mother-in-law negotiated the small flight to the drawing-room door.

'All right, Granny?' he shouted after her.

Mealtimes were the most difficult. Granny ate slowly, prodding at each vegetable several times before finally declaring,

'Got him!' When Richard was there he tried to act normally, asking rather stiffly, 'Granny, what would you like to drink?' before my father quickly chipped in on her behalf.

'Granny has water. From the mains. Awful cloudy stuff now too.'

Barbara Barton, on the other hand, had settled in easily. Though elderly herself and now sporting a septic foot, she lurched about the kitchen quite happily, and her cocky, jubilant Cumbrian accent brought a refreshing note of vitality into the household.

'Don't go biting Barbara now,' she told the dogs excitedly as she gave them their supper. 'No snatchin'. No snatchin'!' she said, her voice rising to a crescendo.

When she was not cooking, she sat solidly in an armchair reading the local Cumberland newspaper. In the evening, she kept to the routines of the past.

'I'll just make up your gran's hot bottle,' she said promptly at seven o'clock.

It was easier for everyone when the better weather came and my grandmother could go into the garden on her own. Dressed in a fetching woollen helmet and carrying her silver-topped walking stick, she tilted along the pathways at a surprising speed and then suddenly stopped, put her hands to her waist and uttered a croaky cough.

After a few weeks, my father seemed to have come to terms with his paying guest.

'D'you know something?' he remarked one night after his mother-in-law had gone to bed. 'Granny thoroughly enjoys some gossip.'

Instead, he lashed out at his eldest son.

'Richard is a Quakerly man. Deadly dull to a lot of people. He would make a good prison governor. I've always said that.'

And, as always, there were the dogs to tease.

'Last night I made Gilda take one of my cod liver oil pills. She was very suspicious about it.'

*

The disbanding of my grandmother's house had been tactfully delayed till after her departure and was then accomplished with such rapidity that certain longed-for items never turned up. I became the owner of my grandmother's long run of *Punch*, but wondered what had happened to the chiming clock. My mother was distressed by the disappearance of her father's fishing things.

'I suppose Granny sold them fifty years ago. A lot of things were sold. All I've got is his box of salmon flies and his reel.'

Now at last Aunt Peg was able to make her own move, and shortly afterwards my mother telephoned her at her new abode.

'Hello? Peg? A good moment to catch you? Two nice nights and all went well? Has Armstrong got a job? Granny wants to know if Armstrong has got a job.'

Later I heard my aunt say, 'Goodbye, my dear. Thank you for ringing up.'

*

I soon paid Aunt Peg a weekend visit. Her single-storey cottage was up a muddy lane and was itself half sunk in the ground. Into it my aunt had squeezed a great deal of furniture from my grandmother's house, including a surprising number of beds. There were two in the kitchen, two in the sitting room and three in an outhouse.

'I can sleep seven,' she explained.

The idea was that her five nephews and other more distant

relations could all come and stay at once, a highly unlikely event especially since Aunt Amy's will had apparently divided the family.

The disorder of Peg's old bedroom in my grandmother's house now extended throughout her cottage. County Council papers floated about in each room and an old letter from my father – 'Ben started work last week in the kitchens of the Dorchester Hotel. It will indeed be hard work' – lay smudged and wet on the bathroom window sill. There were many bottlenecks to squeeze through and obstacles to duck under, including a long string across the kitchen at eye level from which hung various cards, messages and pictures, an old photograph of myself as a professional comedian, and some new coloured snapshots of Edward and Michiko's wedding feast. Peg was a devoted aunt and the first member of the family to express total delight at my brother's marriage. She was counting the days to their visit to England – now only a few weeks away – and was thrilled that they had promised to come and stay with her.

Aunt Peg was equally overjoyed by her new home. 'The first night I got into bed, I was thrilled. I could hardly believe I was doing it. I had thought about it for so long.'

She apparently had few fond memories of her long life with my grandmother. 'I led a worm's life. Granny thought I had to be checked in all sorts of ways, like a baby. Sometimes I was goaded beyond endurance . . .'

Now she could live as she liked. She wore pyjamas most of the time, ate meals at odd hours and did not seem to notice when the cats she had brought with her snatched bits of food off her plate or clawed at the jars of home-made jam on the kitchen table.

The weekend was spend playing chess, Peg crouching on

the leather humpty beside the fireplace while rain pattered against the windows and calves and bullocks bellowed outside. Between moves, we talked about my parents and brothers – 'Richard is a very interesting person and I wish he'd go into politics . . . Your mother is my closest confidante . . .' – but soon the conversation drifted back to my grandmother and her once formidable character.

'I think Ben has inherited Granny's practical side. Granny would have run a hotel splendidly,' said Peg. It was only when she was eighty-seven that Granny showed signs of beginning to fail. Up till five years ago, Granny could still chair meetings.'

In spite of the extreme informality of the household, my aunt spoke sharply when I entered her bedroom without knocking – 'Don't come in. I'm changing' – and summoning me to eat some fried bacon and apple at 2.45 on Saturday afternoon she had the nerve to call out crisply, 'Luncheon!'

On Sunday, Peg and I made our way across three water-logged fields to a little sandstone church where we sat in the back row. After the service, my aunt pointed out my grandfather's grave and introduced me to two old women who had once worked as housemaids for my grandmother and who seemed to smile and stare as if they considered us both – to use Peg's own expression – 'a little on the queer side'.

Little dramas went on throughout the weekend and were sometimes brought about by my aunt's short-sightedness as well as her inexperience at running a home. 'I've put salt in my tea!' she exclaimed one Sunday afternoon, but by the end of my visit it was quite obvious that Aunt Peg had found happiness at last.

10

My father still made occasional trips to London. He came up for the dentist or passed through on his way home after a golfing tour. 'Father rang up,' said Ben one evening. 'He wants me to have tea with him tomorrow.'

Another summer afternoon he had arranged to meet me at Charing Cross Station, where he would be arriving from Sandwich. He was the last off the train. A porter carried his two holdalls, which he had always preferred to conventional suitcases. He held his own golf clubs and an old Burberry. His face seemed surprisingly suntanned, flushed with health, as he advanced towards the ticket barrier.

We went to the station cafeteria where his unconventional request – 'Tea please, double milk' – did not upset the lady behind the counter, and he then took the Underground to Paddington.

A few days after my visit to Aunt Peg, I met him again, this time for lunch at the Reform Club. Our meeting had a difficult beginning – he yelped my name on the doorstep – but the grand old building had a calming effect on him and his old blue pin-striped suit lent him a certain swagger.

'When I came here regularly I knew quite a lot of people,' he said. Now of course I know nobody.' But when we had taken our seats in the long dining room at the back of the building, my father said in a low voice, 'The waiter does know me.'

During lunch, my father imitated my grandmother eating, the fork going into his cheek.

'Granny loves me being away. Absolutely adores my being in London.'

Afterwards he showed me a library where a lot of old men lay snoring. Some looked very old indeed, on the point of death.

'Of course the club is at its busiest now,' said my father.

Over coffee in the gallery upstairs, he then talked of Edward and his Japanese bride – and their imminent arrival in England. He supposed that they would take 'a furnished flat in London' during their visit – 'and then tour Europe in a hired car. He did not want them staying in Wiltshire for weeks on end – except of course on a commercial basis'.

*

Before seven one November morning Richard, Ben and I drove to Heathrow Airport to meet our brother and sister-in-law off a British Airways flight from Tokyo.

It was two and a half years since we had seen Edward.

'There's a lot he's got to be filled in on,' murmured Ben as we waited for them to emerge from the Customs Hall, and I learnt later that Richard had already attempted to begin this process by writing Edward a long letter about how England had changed. 'The satire era is over. *Private Eye* is a thing of the past,' he had written. 'Nobody makes jokes like that any more.'

The first thing that struck me was that my brother was more than a foot taller than his bride. Michiko was tiny, smiling, with a large round face and baby's complexion. Edward was unchanged except for his gold-framed spectacles, and he lumbered behind his bride with a half-smile on his face. Neither of them seemed tired by the long night flight across the world.

During the car journey back into London – we were all squeezed into Richard's Volkswagen – Michiko played with the brass chain on her handbag and said very little. Ben left the party at Notting Hill Gate – he was on an early shift at the Dorchester – but the rest of us drove to Richard's house where Sally had prepared breakfast. Edward and his bride then left for Paddington and the Bristol Pullman and there was a brief post mortem.

Sally had noticed that Michiko dominated my brother. Richard said, 'We must teach her Harrods.'

Edward had lost none of his abruptness, but there was evidence that he was reaping the rewards of working abroad. Cameras and other consumer goods were among his luggage. His white tailor-made shirt had a high collar and unusual curved cuffs – and there was a glint of determination and the beginnings of jowls on his jaw. Beside him Richard looked pale and tired.

*

The following weekend, I was not surprised to find that the ice had completely broken between my father and his new daughter-in-law.

'Koko is a most excellent provider,' he declared after she had cooked his breakfast one morning. He was also delighted with Edward's obvious prosperity and progress in the bank.

'Edward's-going-to-be-managing-director!' he chanted.

My mother and her new daughter-in-law got on well from the start and I found them arranging in order of preference the Christmas cards which were now beginning to arrive. A hideous card depicting a drunken reindeer and inscribed in red ink 'To you all Love Bobbie' my mother pronounced to be 'bottom' and a card from a hospital board colleague showing a new hospital was described as 'second- bottom'.

Michiko's respect for my parents, veneration for my grand-mother and special affection for the rest of us, was rather shaming. She made no comment on the uncomfortable arrangements, the ricketiness of the central heating system or the fumes with which it had now begun to fill the house, all of which were subjects for endless comment from the rest of us.

*

A few days later, my brother Tim arrived unexpectedly in England. Though he sent a flow of letters and postcards from abroad, his movements were always unpredictable 'Have you any idea when Tim is coming?' my mother asked hopelessly from time to time.

Now he was here at last – and in a new Fiat van paid for, he said, from the proceeds of an exhibition in Florence. Tim had found a style of life that suited him. He did not appear to take his work particularly seriously, but he loved the life of an artist, loved setting up his easel on street corners in elegant cities and was extremely industrious and productive, capable of turning out three or four paintings a week. As these were not introspective or experimental but attractive, sunny and modestly priced, he was able to sell them almost as quickly as he could paint them.

He had begun in his mid-teens, painting local views during the holiday – his first 'commission' had come from the cleaning lady, who had paid him ten shillings for a picture of her cottage. His spell as a picture restorer – my father had insisted that he obtain some basic qualification – was brief, and for the past seven or eight years he had supported himself as an artist. He now had friends and patrons all over the place and painted portraits, landscapes, country houses and anything else people wanted. The only subjects he disliked were dogs and horses, though he was sometimes required to include these in the background of portraits of their owners.

Painting was his first love. Now twenty-nine years old, he

had shown no signs of marrying but there were many women in his life and his letters from abroad often made an oblique allusion to some girl currently sharing part of his life.

'Tim leads a much more exciting life than I do,' Richard had recently remarked wistfully.

Although Tim had long ago left Richard behind in a certain sense, he remained loyal to his elder brother and defended him that winter against my occasional criticism.

'But Richard gives you lots of advice and help.'

Tim's prolonged absences from the family circle, his continuing survival in a glamorous profession, had allowed him to escape the dragging down effect of proximity to my father – the responsibilities of which seemed to weigh so heavily on Richard's shoulders, had driven Ben into his shell and had perhaps caused me to shout in my sleep. Tim also had a streak of self-protective cattiness which enabled him to keep the upper hand over his siblings. 'What's the trouble, William? Your mind is wandering. Have another drink,' was followed by a more lively line of attack, 'Have you been sick in that coat? No? You could have fooled me.'

It was typical that he did not immediately go home that winter but spent at least a week in London, opening up his studio in Chelsea and renewing his friendships. He had only to walk a few yards down King's Road to meet people he knew, acquire new invitations and with them the promise of further commissions.

Eventually he drove home to receive a chorus of congratulation and welcome from all concerned – and unintentionally steal the limelight which Edward and Michiko had been enjoying.

'Tim is now the most successful painter of his age in South-West England,' said my father, who loved to speak in superlatives however qualified.

There were also incomprehensible murmurs of approval from his new Japanese sister-in-law, croaks of delight from his grandmother and mutters of contentment from my mother. Though she would never admit it, Tim was my mother's favourite son. She loved him for 'his charming, easy self' and in several respects he was the closest to her in character.

Even now, though he was finally home, Tim avoided the worst of domestic claustrophobia by going out painting at all opportunities and in all weathers. Nobody complained when he arrived hours late for lunch, carrying his latest picture and placing it carefully on the dining-room sideboard before sitting down to a meal by himself, my father dancing attendance.

'Tim can finish the claret. He's not here very often.'

*

That year Richard had chosen to spend Christmas with his in-laws but the rest of us were together in Wiltshire. Even Aunt Peg had been persuaded to leave her new home to spend the festive season with us – and was soon squawking happily at my mother. Ben was the last to arrive – kept working late on Christmas Eve – and he and I shared the icy double bedroom at the back of the house which we had occupied as children.

'This isn't funny,' said my younger brother, getting into bed wearing his overcoat and then addressing the dog that had tangled itself up in the blankets. 'Tiggywinkle, dear, has the hot-water bottle burst? Tigger's given me an apple pie bed!'

A distant slam of doors told us that my father had still not gone to bed.

'Father's downstairs doing a Slow Mile,' said Ben.

*

My father was proud to have so many of his family around him
– at church on Christmas Day we filled two pews. Barbara Barton
alone remained at home. Michiko sat beside my father. I sat next
to my brother Edward and noticed that when the collection came
round both he and Tim put in five-pound notes – and with none
of the exaggerated rustlings and attention-seeking delays that
always accompanied my father's donations.

Later, my father complained that the church was cold. 'The
Lord didn't want us to go and worship Him in conditions
like that. There are miles of pipes in that church. None of
them working,' he said as the more active of us walked home.

My grandmother was the first back to the fireside and was
sitting there spreading out her fingers and stroking the red
flesh when I entered the room.

'We've got a good fire on,' she said cordially.

In a stage whisper, Aunt Peg then talked about the Christmas
presents she was giving.

'I'm giving Granny a nightgown. But she doesn't know yet.'

When lunch began, my father was still talking about the
coldness of the church.

'How the devil they keep a place like Winchester or Salisbury
or Canterbury warm I don't know.'

As one course followed another, some prepared by Ben and
Michiko, my father remarked, 'Tomorrow, it'll be simple fare.
Obviously.'

After lunch I wandered into my father's study and found
my younger brother on the telephone to his girl-friend.

'Private call. Please leave the room,' he said.

Presents were then unwrapped. My grandmother struggled
for ages to unwrap each parcel and then asked politely, 'When
are we having tea?'

My father gave each member of the family the same present

– an engagement diary. He did this every year, buying them in bulk and hurling them out without wrapping them up. Even Barbara was the recipient of one of these gifts and put on her spectacles to study it carefully.

Sooner or later, my father drew one of his sons aside. 'Tim and I want to have a private talk,' he said, and he was still going full tilt twenty minutes later. 'Captain Rogers didn't turn up at the first meeting. Dr Brown was bloody cross . . . Colonel Cocky's been ill and I have given him a bottle of sherry . . . My speech to the Football Club went down very well . . .'

With the swagger of someone constantly on the move, Tim drew nonchalantly on a cigarette and then screened himself behind a paperback about the American Civil War. Occasionally he would murmur, 'Poor Mother!'

As the day continued, the family became more fragmented. Peg, Ben and I paid court to my grandmother beside the fire.

'What's that out there?' she asked as Michiko bobbed past the window in a padded jacket.

'D'you know what time it is?' she asked for the third or fourth time. 'Time you had a watch,' said Ben in a low voice.

'What?'

'D'you know where your mother is?' she asked again while Aunt Peg began in another stage whisper, 'Granny doesn't like me. She loves me but she doesn't like me and she finds it exasperating.'

At about six o'clock Richard telephoned from the Sussex farmhouse where he was spending Christmas with his in-laws.

'How's Sam? How's Tessie?' asked my mother. 'Good. Good. Richard, my dear, we're missing you all.'

In the evening we watched television and the conversation branched out onto broader, lighter topics.

'Dora Bryan drinks practically nothing,' said my father. 'I know because I've seen her on the Brighton train.'

Christmas Day ended with a report from Ben that my mother had fallen asleep in her bath – 'Absolutely sound asleep.'

Boxing Day began with my mother asking Edward, 'Are you tired of boiled eggs?' and Edward replying, 'Not in the least, no.'

For once there was superficial harmony between my father and Aunt Peg.

'Peg got the telly yet?' he asked in a rhetorical and over-bearing manner, but when she set off to her new home two days later he said, 'Goodbye, Peg. Come again whenever you want.'

After she had gone, however, he made a joke at her expense. 'Peg's gone back to Cumberland. Bloody good thing too. For Cumberland,' and soon I found him writing a letter to his absent eldest son.

'Your aunt is now noticeably deafer. In addition to all her other troubles which we have known about so long.'

11

Six weeks later, Edward and Michiko returned to the Far East. Their visit to England had been a great success and the weekend in Aunt Peg's cottage one of the trip's highlights.

'Michiko's fallen in love with Cumberland,' Edward had told my mother on the telephone.

'Good,' my mother had replied.

Tim also went on his way – arranging to visit Edward and Michiko in the Far East later in the year and begging his brothers who remained in England to write to him more often. His parting shot, or threat, to me was of a humorous nature.

'If you're still wearing that coat, William, next time I see you . . .' With the departure of these globe-trotters, life fell back into its old pattern. At home, the central heating was turned off. Relations died. 'Cousin Archie's Funeral' was the main topic of conversation one weekend. This flashy figure, who had also abandoned Quakerism, was to have a memorial service in a London church. 'Ticket holders only . . . God Almighty!' said my father as he read the announcement in *The Times*. In February, the odd battered primrose appeared in the garden and my parents' thirtieth wedding anniversary – 'We probably won't get to Gold' – passed without any exchange of gifts.

'Foreign people celebrate anniversaries. We don't,' said my father flatly.

One weekend I tried to stir things up by revealing that I had been seeing a psychiatrist. To prove it, I took out a bill from a Harley Street shrink and waved it in front of Richard and my father, both of whom tried to dodge the issue in their own ways.

'I want to see the cash amount,' shouted Richard excitedly.

My father reacted in his most high and mighty hospital board manner: 'I shall look into this very carefully with the BMA on Monday morning.'

In fact he did nothing at all about it and I wasn't even sure if he had really taken in what I was saying.

The main burden on the household was now my grandmother. Her rapid deterioration had a depressing effect on all of us.

'I remember Granny when she was intelligent and amusing,' said Richard.

'Granny is very tedious,' conceded Ben. 'She's so old.'

A few weeks later it was my turn to be annoyed when my grandmother made some remark to the effect that she thought I was still working as a comedian. My fierce over-reaction drew a rebuke from Ben, who was reading a book in the corner.

'OK, so she goofed,' he murmured. 'Forget it.'

It was far worse for my mother, who had to spend more and more time sitting with the old lady by the fire and felt obliged to follow her if she decided to wander into the garden.

'Can't you let her go out on her own sometimes?' I asked.

'And grease the top of the steps?' replied my father, drumming his fingers on the table and trying to catch my eye.

*

Later in the Spring, I found my mother sunk deep in a chair, suffering from something more serious than fatigue. Suddenly she blurted out to me, 'My mind is addled. I always knew it would be bad but it's much worse than I imagined.'

All my mother's life she had regarded my grandmother as 'an old dear'. Now at last she saw her limitations and had begun to look upon her as 'a very good, but very dull old woman'.

'I would be quite happy aged ninety tending my plants and fondling my dogs,' she said. 'I'm seriously thinking of making a signed statement that I'll never live with any of you.'

One of the main sacrifices my mother had made on my grandmother's behalf was her fishing. In the old days she had gone off two or three days a week to fish in local streams, rivers and reservoirs. Now she had not touched her rods for months.

'I think, talk and dream fishing,' she said in despair, 'I don't give a damn about the garden. It's the fishing.'

My father, who had become ruder and ruder to his mother-in-law – 'We know all that Granny. We're not at school now' – made a grim little speech one night in the kitchen about my mother's health after she had gone to bed.

These speeches now occurred with increasing frequency and my father had recently reminded my mother of a time, long ago, when she had nearly died.

'Rather a good thing if I had,' she had replied uncharacteristically, drawing a harshly indignant response from my father.

That night in the kitchen my father was full of unctuous altruism. 'Of course the most serious thing,' he said gravely, 'is her fishing.' Then he added a wicked exaggeration. 'Of course she can't abide having Granny here. Poor old thing, nobody wants her.'

12

Meanwhile, Ben and I had had a change of accommodation in London. The lease in South Kensington had expired and by a happy chance the flat Tim had acquired below his studio had been vacated. After some deliberation, Tim had decided to let us take it over and telephoned us to this effect from abroad. This was partly a gesture of brotherly loyalty and partly because he thought we would be easier to push around than people he knew less well. He also hoped we would be able to keep an eye on his precious studio during his long absences, and deal with his commissions and invitations.

Hiring a van, which Ben drove with supreme confidence, we moved our goods and chattels, including the bound volumes of *Punch* from my grandmother's house, across

Chelsea and heaved them up the broad staircase to the second-floor flat. Our new home was in a building with historic associations. Whistler – or was it Augustus John? – had once occupied the studio above us while downstairs there now lived and worked a fashionable young tailor whose clients included the Rolling Stones.

Ben quickly imposed his familiar routines on the place. 'Perishing cold,' he remarked one night as he made up his hot-water bottle.

Another night when I requested the use of the hot-water bottle myself, he did not seem to hear but later entered the room and hurled an object onto my bed.

'Here she is!' he cried.

Tensions between us were more marked than in our previous abode – and even the catering arrangements did not run smoothly. Sometimes I found Ben munching an apple from a secret store. Sometimes there was a smell of fried bacon lingering in the flat.

'Could you make some coffee?' I suggested one evening.

'Possibly,' he replied.

Things came to a head a few weeks after we took up residence when I recklessly opened a letter addressed to him by Mary York.

As usual, Ben suppressed his feelings and, instead of shouting angrily, simply stood looking at me with one eye and half a smile, holding his stare for an abnormal length of time.

Soon after this, I tried to tease him about the mundane nature of his work at the hotel.

'Do you still have to clock in?'

'Everybody clocks in except for managers, and you know I'm not a manager.'

My own career was nothing to boast about. In fact, I had recently been demoted at the advertising agency and assigned to menial and unimportant tasks. 'Just carry on quietly doing what you are told,' my father advised me in a letter. 'The essential thing is to part on good terms and be able to produce some sort of reference.'

The dreariness of my situation was emphasised by an improvement in Ben's life.

'Oh, do tell me Ben's good news,' pleaded my mother, to whom he had hinted that something was afoot.

In the summer of 1969, my younger brother suddenly turned his back on the hotel business and sailed effortlessly into a copywriting job in a much more illustrious advertising firm than my own. Here, he was apparently hailed as a brilliant new talent and he could soon regale me with gripping stories about his workmates, making them sound far more amusing than my own.

One morning, soon after he had started in the new firm, I woke to hear my brother groaning and yelping as he vomited into the lavatory bow.

'Christ, you're ill!' I said.

I later telephoned his firm on his behalf and spoke to a girl in his office.

'Give him my love,' she said, 'and tell him to get better soon.'

13

On the eve of her ninetieth birthday my grandmother fell out of her bed. A few days later, she fell out again. A doctor was called, then a specialist.

'You'll notice a change in her,' said my mother when she collected me from the station.

That evening I found my grandmother struggling with a boiled egg.

'This is senility of an extreme kind,' said my father.

'The specialist said it could be two hours. It could be ten years,' said my mother.

'I'm getting feebler,' said Granny herself.

Barbara Barton was also in a decline. Her septic foot was now so heavily bandaged that you could not make out its outline and a tall stool was introduced into the kitchen which Barbara could sit upon or lean against as she dabbed at the stove or work surfaces with her all-purpose cloth – or leant forward to give the dogs their supper.

'Her foot is oozing pus,' said my father. 'I think she's going to collapse and simply say she can't go on.'

A few weeks later, Barbara was admitted to a local hospital – 'One of mine,' my father added proudly. Telephone conferences between various parties then took place – with the outcome that my grandmother should now return to Cumberland. A place was soon secured for her in a state-run old folk's home near her former village where by a strange coincidence her old employee Armstrong was working as a porter. A suggestion heroically extended by Aunt Peg that Granny should go and live with her once again had been dismissed by everybody as 'surely not a good idea', not only because of the obvious unsuitability of the house but also because Aunt Peg herself had recently begun to find life difficult.

'Peg's always falling down,' my mother had reported. 'She fell down inspecting a caravan site. One of the caravans took

78

her in and made her lie down. She had to soak her stocking off. It was stuck with blood.'

My grandmother's removal to Cumberland took place promptly – Barbara Barton was to follow her to the same establishment a few weeks later. My grandmother's car – the well-kept Morris Minor – was to remain in Wiltshire; my mother had claimed it was a reward for her twenty-two months' hard labour. The furniture was disposed of locally. The silver-topped walking stick, left behind by mistake, would be sent back to Cumberland, my father said gleefully, 'by passenger train'.

14

Letters and postcards arrived regularly from Tim. He wrote them on aeroplanes and in boats, keeping busy even when he was not painting. The trip to the Far East had been a great success. He had stayed with Edward and Michiko at their new home in Bangkok – 'They seem to thrive in the heat' – and gone back to Italy and was now uncertain when he would next be in London. 'I wish you could be with me to share all this fun,' he wrote.

From time to time I still saw Richard in London. He and Sally still hated to pick up the telephone, which got each conversation off to a bad start.

One day Richard had answered, 'Look, William, we're in the middle of lunch.'

Another time, Sally informed me that Richard was out, visiting our old school. 'He's gone up to Speech Day,' she explained.

I had never re-visited the place, but Richard, whose pole-vault record was still unbroken, enjoyed returning to the scenes of his early triumphs. 'He'll be back at eight o'clock,' Sally added.

Eventually I would get through to my sibling and we would chat in the usual constricted manner. Sometimes I thought I could hear my sister-in-law saying something hostile in the background. Invitations were extended, withdrawn, altered and re-extended. Eventually a dinner date was changed to lunch – 'so you can see the children' – and in the middle of a storm I found myself ringing my brother's doorbell for the first time for over a year.

'Haven't you got a coat? You're mad!' was his opening remark.

'I'm very tough.'

'Nasty day,' said Sally.

'I like your new hairstyle,' said Richard. 'Makes you look younger. Improves you.'

Lunch was served and wine was opened. The conversation soon turned to family matters.

'Ben's had it drummed into him that he's not bright. By all sorts of people,' said Richard.

'Father's been bored by Mummy for the last twenty years,' he declared. 'He must get very lonely sitting there with her. We must go home as often as possible.'

Sally served the pudding and withdrew to the next room leaving us together at the table.

'My wife doesn't like my parents,' Richard said, offering me a cigarette.

'Go and look at Tessie in her baby bouncer before you go,' he said, getting up.

'I must say. I'm exhausted. I need a holiday,' he said as I set off again.

A few days later, I happened to pass the house again and in a moment of high spirits decided to ring the bell. I saw Sally's face moving behind the curtains but she did not answer the door and I walked away feeling hollow in the stomach.

*

Meanwhile, Ben had taken up a new interest. With an urgency I could not understand, he had begun painting and drawing. His pictures bore no resemblance to Tim's easy-on-the-eye canvases, about which – though these two brothers got on well enough together – he was vindictively dismissive. But Ben was now equally scornful of established Old Masters. One Saturday we visited the National Gallery together and inspected Constable's Flatford Mill.

'It's frightfully bad!' said Ben.

His own work featured decapitated corpses, weeping faces, accidents of all sorts, a mass of blood and tears, scribbles and split ink which sharply contrasted with his own tidy appearance. The concentration he applied to it was remarkable. Within moments of his return to the flat he would be hunched over his desk, calmly and steadily working at his latest pen-and-ink drawing. From the next room I could hear an occasional sniff and the squeak of his nib as it moved across the paper.

Using every spare quarter hour in this way, Ben was now less likely than ever to be found flopped in an armchair or leafing through a magazine. Our own conversations were increasingly monosyllabic and more often than not he would reject any diversion I might suggest – 'I'm not sure if I do, actually' – claiming again and again that it was more profitable to work. Ben framed his pictures himself and acquired a small brown attaché case in which to carry resin, chalks, chisels, sticky brown paper and other tools of his new hobby.

On Saturday mornings, Ben would go off to visit glass merchants, artists' supply shops and galleries. Within a few weeks, he had sold a picture to a gallery in Cork Street.

*

While Ben's life expanded in this way, my own had been contracting. That summer I was sacked from my job after thirty months' service. I was now marooned in the flat while Ben was more and more out and about. His social programme had become increasingly busy. Many weekends he would have crossed England before I had stirred from my bed. I would listen for his return. He had now replaced his grey van with a secondhand red Mini: a popular car at the time, but I soon learnt to recognise its noises as it pulled into a parking space in the street outside, followed a few moments later by Ben's footsteps on the wide stone staircase and the squeak of his hand on the varnished banister.

His visits to the flat were fleeting, His life continued to gather pace. Invitations in stiff white envelopes arrived regularly – sometimes in the same post as rejections of my first attempt at a novel. Though Ben kept his old friend Mary York stringing along, his pocket book was now crammed with the names and telephone numbers of other girls. Many of these new acquaintances seemed to have two homes. Nether Wallop, Midhurst and Towcester addresses were appended to Belgravia and Flaxman numbers. He rarely invited these girls to the flat and avoided telephoning them if I was around. Once I had innocently picked up the phone: he had immediately accused me of listening to a private call and argued in favour of having the extension cut off.

One day that autumn, however, Ben announced that a man he had met at a house party would be coming round for a drink. That evening I met for the first time a thin, pale young man named Jack Pratt.

15

My father's life was even more difficult after my grandmother left. A new wizened expression on his face was matched by the increasing sag of his trousers. Most weekends he spent crashing about the house accusing people of stealing things he had mislaid.

'Now this is a very serious matter. My mackintosh has been stolen,' he shouted.

'Oh, no, it hasn't!' shouted my mother, tying flies again in the back kitchen.

Another time he rushed towards me brandishing a telephone bill. On a separate sheet, listing calls via the operator, he had drawn a furious inky circle round one item.

'Did you make this call?'

At breakfast, lunch and dinner, he was in a querulous, miserable state, grabbing and spitting out food, using the wrong cutlery, hurling insults, will-dangling at every opportunity.

'The older boys get a little more because they are the older boys,' he said in a sing-song voice.

'Who is your girl-friend now?' he asked in a more brutal voice and then repeated his old threat, 'Sons who don't marry get less. That's perfectly obvious.'

'Don't bang that door!' he suddenly screamed at me. 'You might do a thousand pounds worth of damage!'

If I said or did anything that especially annoyed him he had one particular insult up his sleeve.

'You're just like your Aunt Peg,' he would say.

Between meals he vented his anger on the big old-fashioned Rover, which had once been his pride and joy.

'It's never had this trouble before,' he said as he crunched its gears. 'This car's turned out to be a real bad 'un.'

To my mother's dismay, he would occasionally borrow the Morris Minor.

'My life depends on that little car,' she pleaded. 'If you bashed its wing and it had to go to hospital I don't know what I should do.'

Sometimes he would announce, 'I'm off,' but then simply drive the car round to the front door, go inside again and mess around upstairs for a further hour. He might then abandon his plans to go to the local golf club, wander instead into the garden and practise a few desultory shots on his private course.

I dreaded his approach. The sound of his horn on the drive or the creak of the floorboards outside my room at night made me tremble. One evening he entered my room with the stalk of a cigar in his mouth and accused me of stealing one of his ties. Though I denied this he marched out chanting 'Deductio!' which meant he would make an appropriate cut in my small monthly allowance.

Such was his conviction that he was even able to convince my mother of my guilt. 'Father is agitating about a pair of blue pyjamas,' she wrote to me. 'Did you take them?'

Another time my father entered the room where I sat watching television and started staring at the front of my trousers and making cryptic murmurings.

'Those aren't normal contours,' he said thoughtfully and

then, triumphantly switching into his sing-song voice, 'Tommy's not the only dog in the house!'

He continued to defile his environment. Earlier that year he had drained the small lily pond below his bedroom window, having decided that it was 'a breeding ground for every sort of germ'. Now he had arranged for every downstairs window to be fitted with security bolts, making them impossible to open without the master key. He kept this himself – and often lost it.

'Father's not well,' murmured Ben, who now used every spare moment to work on his drawings. Our parents did not disturb him and he remained aloof when my mother protested that he had been doing his 'scribbles' on the best writing paper. When he heard my father ceremoniously counting the letters he was going to post – 'One, two, three, four, five, six, seven letters!' – he chipped in irreverently, 'French letters?' There was a longish silence and then my father asked, 'Was that a drawing-room joke, a conservatory joke, or a smoking-room joke?'

My father had found a new hidey-hole for his bottles of spirits – a locked cupboard under the staircase – and there was much banging and crashing about to find the key whenever he wanted to offer anyone a drink.

When he did relax, it was only to spew out more grim material about the neighbours.

'Dr Brown has made gross allegations about the way in which the last ballot was taken and has accused me of voting against him . . . Oh, by the way, the vicar's health has broken down.'

From time to time he would speculate about my grandmother's new life in the nursing home three hundred miles to the north.

'I hope she's keeping on the right side of Matron,' he said.

Barbara Barton was also the inspiration for some bleak afterthoughts. 'That poor wretched Barbara. She was always making unhealthy food. She was always making batter.'

16

Pale, thin Jack Pratt had no job and thus had plenty of time to pursue his friendships with Ben and me separately. That winter, he would call on me during the day at the flat – 'You smell of decay' – and then go off to lunch with my brother in the West End.

It was during one of these lunches – in a wine bar near Ben's office – that Jack had recognised among the other customers an old schoolmaster he had once known. The man had now fallen on bad times but Jack and Ben had been delighted by him and had invited him to come round to the flat later that day.

Thick snow fell that afternoon and the old man did not reach the flat till ten o'clock at night. He was a small, vintage figure, a little older than my father, but better educated, with a courtly, foppish manner. He wore a worn tweed jacket, shabby check waistcoat and an overcoat, to the collar of which he appeared to have sewn a strip of moth-eaten fur. In spite of these sartorial disadvantages, he was soon talking facetiously over port – and handling his cigarette in a dainty, supercilious manner.

'I deliberately put on this dirty shirt because I thought it was more Chelsea,' he said.

Ben and Jack were delighted by the man's antics and kept his glass full – and the witticisms soon gave way to less articulate utterances, cries for more port and then for the lavatory.

As the night grew longer and colder, he became increasingly reluctant to leave and my brother, apparently flattered by the old man's attentiveness, seemed equally eager that Mr Blunt – this was his name – should stay the night in the flat.

I eventually persuaded Ben to drive his new friend back to his lodgings in the East End. Jack and I travelled in the back of the car for the ride through the snowy streets. At about three in the morning, Mr Blunt dismissed us at a street corner, refusing to reveal his exact address, and Ben repeated his apologies that we could not let him stay the night.

Mr Blunt then glared at me in the back of the car and said, 'It was your decision and yours alone.'

Ben's relationship with Mr Blunt progressed rapidly. Though his life was already quite full, he pursued this friendless old man vigorously over the next few weeks. He kept me informed of the progress of the relationship and sang Blunt's praises.

'He's a shrewd, intelligent man. Not some silly down-and-out in a dirty mac.'

The old man several times tried to escape my brother's attention – and continued to keep his precise address a secret. They met in wine bars, pubs, churches and cafés, and Blunt sent my brother dozens of letters – and then suddenly a postcard fiercely terminating the friendship and blaming Ben for the current crisis in his life.

But my brother was not going to let Blunt get away so easily. 'I just want to put my side of it,' he said and set off to the East End where he left letters for his friend in fourteen different pubs near the corner where we had dropped him that first night.

'Isn't that rather odd?' I asked.

'Blunt knows I'm odd,' he replied.

Within twenty-four hours the old man had telephoned Ben at his office and their strange friendship had been repaired.

'I gave him a quid and a cup of tea,' said Ben after their reunion in a café the same afternoon.

*

Shortly before Christmas 1969 Ben left the flat for good. From now on I saw him only occasionally. I knew little of his movements or whereabouts. The room he had rented down the street was often unoccupied and it was obvious there were other places he preferred to be. On his visits to the flat he was brusque, picking up letters without glancing at them and speeding off.

He continued to keep me informed about Mr Blunt, but I suspected that he was involved in some further relationship. This explanation also appealed to Jack Pratt, who had likewise been excluded from the new phase of my younger brother's life.

'Ben is bitten by the love bug,' Jack pronounced. 'He's putting up a smoke screen between us and his soul.'

On his rare visits home, Ben was even more cagey about his activities in London.

'Now who are you sharing a flat with?' my father began fiercely. 'John Smith,' my younger brother replied playfully.

'Real name, please,' snapped back my father, and soon an argument developed which ended with my mother pleading with Ben that she and my father were only interested in his 'welfare'.

For once my father seemed unconcerned about me. My dismissal by the advertising agency had not surprised him – perhaps he was relieved that his gloomy predictions had been proved right. At any rate he had ceased to harass me about my career, and he sometimes suggested that if things got too tough in London I should simply go and live in Cumberland with Aunt Peg.

17

Early in the New Year, Tim returned to London and Ben reappeared at the flat.

'I've just been helping Tim settle in,' he said.

Though intrigued by his youngest brother's activities, Tim was too busy to give much thought to the matter, and the big studio above my head – silent for many months – began to reverberate to the sounds of an active life. The telephone rang, the piano tinkled or thumped – Tim was the only member of the family with musical aspirations – packing cases were heaved about and a radio and stereo system competed with each other. All day long, Tim's pseudo-military footsteps crossed the ceiling until the evening when I would hear the fall of shoes as my brother hurriedly changed his clothes for a night on the town.

Tim's easygoing qualities that my mother loved so much were widely appreciated – he 'got on' with everyone he met. He had penetrated London life while I was still in my early teens and his knowledge of Kensington and Chelsea went back long before the advent of the Swinging Sixties. Though his world had now expanded and his friends, acquaintances and clients were far further flung, Tim still got on well with his immediate neighbours, the housekeeper in the basement, the trendy tailor and even a dour-faced National Insurance roundsman who called at the studio soon after his return.

There were many visitors to the studio during his brief occupancy, and once or twice a week Tim gave a small, carefully organised party. He usually did not invite me but he boasted afterwards about who had come. 'The So-and-sos are immensely powerful people,' he said with a hint of self mockery. 'Their uncle is Archbishop of Canterbury.'

Tim's amused interest in the ruling classes – snobbery is too strong a word – was not offensive. He was never sycophantic to his clients. Nor did he flatter them in paint. His portraits were unflashy and unglossy; indeed one or two had actually been rejected because the sitter was displeased with the subtle caricature Tim had produced.

In his own way of life he was frugal and self-denying, careful about money, as Quakerish as any of us, a patient plodder, rewarded by the pleasant climates he often worked in and absorbed in his work to the exclusion of most outside irritations. Even Ben's success with his macabre pen-and-ink drawings did not trouble him though he thanked me for taking down a particularly 'silly' one I had hung up in the lavatory – and the other ups and downs of the family did not weigh heavily on his shoulders. He was faithful to Richard and Sally, visiting them often at their house on Campden Hill and chatting effortlessly with them. Only with his parents was he perhaps a little dismissive.

'Father's nearly sixty-three now. I won't go down till the summer,' he said loftily and instead he drove off in other directions, returning to the studio at odd hours, carrying large wet canvases, commissioned work which he would quickly finish off with the aid of photographs.

When eventually he did go home, he came back declaring that Father had been in a bad temper the whole weekend.

'Poor mother!' he sighed.

*

A few weeks after Tim's return to London, Ben at last introduced me to the girl who had claimed so much of his attention. Susi was tall, with a lioness's mane of dark hair and a superbly slender figure. A year older than Ben, she lived in her own flat on Chelsea Green, worked vaguely in interior design and seemed a typical product of the new Swinging London.

After our first meeting, I saw much more of Ben and his girl-friend. Susi, in particular, seemed to welcome me into their world and once or twice that spring I went out with them. They appeared besotted, scribbling love notes to each other even when I was the only other person present. When Susi laughed, she threw back her head with such abandon, showing her handsome jaw and teeth, that I sometimes wondered if she were drugged or drunk. The world they inhabited seemed populated by the fashionable. Ben and Susi were caught up in the final upswing of the 1960s and even received some inaccurate gossip column publicity.

In spite of the attractions of this new world, Ben found time to do his pictures. He also remained deeply attached to Mr Blunt and during that spring had arranged that the old man should stay with him and Susi at the little flat they were sharing on Chelsea Green. This had proved a tricky undertaking. At first Ben seemed delighted with Blunt's misdeeds – 'Susi found Blunt in the kitchen at three in the morning mixing red wine and cider!' – but after a few weeks reported that things had become too difficult.

'Blunt has blotted his copybook,' he told me at the beginning of March. 'He's back to square one on Monday. He hasn't been able to save any money. He comes in and annoys me when I'm working – yes, very like Father. Susi had bronchitis last week and Blunt came in and lay on her bed. He left a smell and a mess in the lavatory this morning. He was walking around in a blanket. If he doesn't earn any money, he'll die.'

This disenchantment with Blunt did not last long and Ben remained his protector, allowing the old schoolmaster to sleep curled up in the back of the little red car.

*

Meanwhile in Wiltshire my father's disappointment with local life had reached a peak. Even charitable work was now in short supply.

'I won't get any more appointments now . . . not at sixty-three,' he said one weekend. 'This place is like a vault, with all of you away and Richard and Edward married.'

The idea of moving to a smaller house in the neighbourhood had once attracted him, but he now ruled it out on the grounds that – my mother explained – it would look as if he had gone down in the world, though many of his contemporaries were making just such a move. A new possibility now occurred to him. Suddenly he had become aware of the huge financial advantages – no death duties and only seventeen per cent income tax – offered by the Isle of Man.

He had never been there and knew little about it other than its benevolent fiscal system, but suddenly he was in love with it and could think of little else. All five sons at first dismissed the scheme as a joke, and my mother expressed horror at the idea of moving to a tax haven which, she felt, was 'ratting' on the government, albeit still a Labour one. During one of my father's exploratory telephone calls to those who might advise him about the move, my mother had rushed from the room cursing whoever my father was talking to. 'Sir Somebody Somebody!' she cried. 'That bloody island!'

The plan was soon under way, however, and a folder bearing

the inky initials 'I.O.M.' was added to the filing cabinet. A wave of fresh sympathy for my mother swept round the neighbourhood but there was no stopping my father.

'Father hates paying tax,' said Tim when he left London that spring for some more congenial clime.

My father's restlessness had suddenly exploded, and for the first time for years he was busy and in a decisive mood. His first step towards his new life was to seek a property on the island and thus begin to establish his 'domicile' as soon as possible. Anywhere would do for this purpose, and in the middle of March my parents flew together to the Isle of Man and made an offer for a tiny white-washed cottage surrounded by golden gorse on the island's most northerly tip. Most reluctantly, my mother had accompanied my father on this trip, but on her return seemed partly reconciled to the idea, perhaps because she had learnt that the fishing on the island was considered quite good.

*

Shortly after their return, Ben told me that he was taking Susi home for the first time and insisted that on no account should I be there the same weekend.

The following week, Ben telephoned me and said that he and Susi were getting married. I may have been one of the last to learn this news. Tim was abroad but Richard, I learned later, had been closely involved in this development.

'We're putting it in the paper next week,' Ben continued. 'Where are you going to live?'

'We'll probably get a little house.'

At home, the news had been greeted with excitement and temporarily shifted attention away from my father's great new project. My mother was pleased to learn that Susi was an

experienced horse-woman – riding had been my mother's principal interest before she had taken up fishing – and my father
was delighted to learn that his prospective daughter-in-law
claimed descent from some ancient North Country families.

'Susi is, as I rather thought might be the case, descended
from very old Catholic county families on both sides,' he
wrote to Aunt Peg, whom he seemed to regard as the family's
archivist.

He was also writing a letter to Susi herself confirming his
arrangement to have lunch with her the following week, an
appointment which would be sandwiched between the dentist
and 'a meeting with a solicitor who specialises in advising
people who are going to live abroad permanently'.

The following week, an announcement appeared in the
Forthcoming Marriages column in *The Times*, giving my
parents' address in full but saying nothing about the whereabouts of Susi's mother and father.

Meanwhile, Ben and Susi sailed around London in an even
more relaxed mood and were full of plans for the wedding,
which was to take place at the end of April at the Brompton
Oratory.

'With any luck your turn will come,' said Jack Pratt, who
discussed the engagement with me at some length, occasionally
muttering that it was 'a rum do'.

The engagement had coincided with a further upset in the
life of Mr Blunt. According to Ben, a man had been murdered
in the hostel to which Blunt had returned in East London
and which had long been his secret home. Blunt had been
questioned about this death at some length – and even Ben
had been interviewed by detectives at his office. Blunt had
later been eliminated from the enquiries and transferred to
a hostel in Oxford. Ben had bought him a first-class ticket

and seen him off at Paddington. Blunt now wore many of my brother's cast-off clothes and said he would not be attending the wedding, partly for fear of being recognised in them by my father.

*

At the beginning of April, Tim was back in England, and he spent his first weekend in Wiltshire with Ben and Susi as fellow guests. He returned to London vaguely displeased about the engagement and uneasy about the relationship.

'Susi needs security. Ben doesn't,' he said at first – and then, 'They just look at each other the whole time thinking about sex. I'm all in favour but – I caught him flashing at her on the stairs.'

The engagement had also gone down badly with Ben's old girlfriend Mary York. At a party in Chelsea which I had attended, Ben and his fiancée had made a late arrival. Mary's face had suddenly filled with blood and she had hurled her champagne glass at his feet. She had then hurtled from the room.

'Go after her,' I ordered, but I now had no power over my younger brother and he made no attempt to do so.

'This has happened before,' he said. 'She only does it to get attention.'

Susi appeared unflustered by this incident and circulated among the other guests like a film star.

*

Tim's return to England was followed by that of my old advertising colleague, Peter Cooper. He had spent most of the last year abroad, had done well for himself and now had better clothes, footwear and a saucy silver sportscar. On his second evening in London, Peter had dinner with Ben and his fiancée.

'She made me nervous,' he said the next morning, 'I couldn't eat and things.'

In the spirit of the moment, I invited him to spend the next weekend in Wiltshire.

'Peter Cooper,' my mother repeated the name unsteadily on the telephone, but the following Saturday we set off in the silver car.

'This is like Turindorf, Germany,' he said as we headed west.

*

My father shot me a mischievous look as he shook hands with Peter, but they were soon talking together politely. My father translated every sum he mentioned into dollars for Peter's benefit.

'Is there any soccer played in America?' asked my father.

'Just a little privately, I think,' said Peter.

Soon all my father's favourite topics had been touched upon, money, wayward nuns, health.

'If you're ill in an American hotel with, say, peritonitis, you may be left to die,' said my father.

Peter was a good listener, and soon my father said, 'I like this chap you've brought down. He's a very nice fellow.'

Then he went outside and started mowing the lawn for the first time that year. Peter and I sat in the drawing room listening to the buzz of the machine.

'God, look at the sky!' he exclaimed. 'It gets misty round here, huh?'

He crouched to light a cigarette off the electric fire. At dinner my father tried to make a harmless joke at my expense – 'My own feeling is that an American military school might have been the best place for William. Some sort of junior

West Point' – but when the meal was over he offered us both cigars.

Peter was soon blowing perfect smoke rings at my father. The following morning, he appeared after I had already had breakfast.

My mother told me to ask my friend if he would like tea or coffee. 'Don't just presume he wants coffee. He may prefer tea.'

Soon after breakfast my father attempted to shut his study door in my face.

'Peter and I want to have a private talk.'

*

I got back to the flat at six that night. It was surprisingly warm for April. Tim had already returned from wherever he had been and I could hear his feet scraping the ceiling. I felt restless. I telephoned the flat on Chelsea Green but there was no reply. I then went up to the studio but Tim was talking on the telephone in his little lobby off the main room, the door half shut.

Soon after I returned to my desk, I heard Tim's footsteps on the staircase.

'William?' he asked as he entered the flat.

'Yes?'

'Prepare yourself for the worst possible news,' he said. 'Ben and Susi have been killed in a car crash.'

18

There was a buzz in the air, an electric feeling I have never experienced before or since. I got up from my desk and leant against a chest. All I could think about was Ben's impishness and impudence. Had he pulled off the ultimate trick? Was it a brilliant hoax?

Tim picked up a cushion and flung it down at the white brick surround of the fireplace. He said something about a nightmare and that he was going immediately to Richard's house.

I said feebly, 'I'll spend the evening with Peter Cooper.'

My old colleague arrived a few minutes later, entering the flat with a profoundly quizzical expression on his face.

'Have you flipped your top?' were his first words.

We then rang the flat on Chelsea Green and the phone was answered by a Yorkshire lady, a friend of Susi's, who Ben had said 'knows everybody in London'. I broke the news clumsily to her – I had hardly taken it in myself – and caused her to go distraught.

I sent Peter to console her and thinking this might not be adequate, ran through the streets after him. When I reached the small top-floor flat, the Yorkshire lady was sitting on the floor talking on the telephone.

My appearance must have told her that this was no hoax because she immediately told the person she was talking to, 'It's true.'

She offered me a sip of whisky from a communal glass, and after a while, a cigarette.

'I think its ciggy time,' she said. No amount of shock could apparently dislodge this curious ritualistic social phrase from her lips.

Later Peter accompanied me back to the flat and spent the night there. As I climbed into my bed, I tried to cry but the tears would not come.

*

Richard and Tim had driven home at once to be with my parents. The next day they were back in London briefly, then set off to Newport Pagnell in Buckinghamshire to identify the bodies and obtain details of the crash.

I soon learned that Ben and his fiancée had been killed in a collision on a country road in broad daylight. Ben had died at once, Susi on the way to hospital. The little red car had been smashed to pieces.

Richard and Tim had also visited the scene of the crash and had found spent morphine cartridges by the roadside. They returned to London with a bag of my brother's possessions, including his cylindrical silver cuff-links.

Meanwhile I had begun to tell various people the news. Some already knew. Others refused to believe me. Jack Pratt, to whom I spoke at his office – he now had a job in the City – said instantly, 'I'm absolutely heartbroken.' At eight o'clock that evening the telephone rang and I heard Mr Blunt struggling to speak to me from Oxford but he was too overcome with emotion.

Throughout, Peter Cooper remained at my side and shared with me the slow sinking feeling that had supplanted the initial electric reaction.

'The novelty's worn off,' he remarked during our second evening together in the flat.

'Have you completely ruled out the possibility of a gigantic practical joke?' I asked.

'Not quite.'

The following day, Tim and I went to the flat on Chelsea Green and gathered up Ben's possessions.

In a sort of trance, and without speaking to each other, we packed into boxes his suits, ties, unframed pictures, alarm clocks, old telegrams, invitations, stone carvings and several books, including Muybridge's *Human Figure in Motion* and Foxe's *Book of Martyrs*.

*

My social circle was still small. I received few messages of sympathy. My mother wrote that she was trying to think of them happy together. An old school contemporary wrote of the tragedy that had 'overtaken' our family, and from the Church Army Hostel at Oxford came the first of a series of letters from Mr Blunt.

'Words fail me re all this,' he began and went on to describe Ben as the son or grandson he had never had and stressed the innocence of the relationship – 'All the fools who looked askance were looking well up the wrong tree.'

A second letter followed in the next post in which Blunt added a request: 'There are some shirts somewhere, a suit and laundry he was retrieving for me. I feel ghoulish writing about them but as this was all his wish it is a shame to lose them.'

Meanwhile, Peter Cooper had also struck a slightly selfish note by asking for the return of three pounds which I had borrowed from him before the tragedy.

*

Requiem Mass for my brother and his fiancée was arranged to take place the following Tuesday at the Brompton Oratory. I went home for the intervening weekend. Both my parents met me at the station and my father drove the eight miles extremely slowly and with exaggerated care. This solemnity soon melted and at the end of the day he was dispensing cigars and saying, 'Ben wouldn't want us to starve, would he?'

My mother had drawn some comfort from an encounter with a squirrel on the day after Ben's death. 'I was sitting in the kitchen when it jumped onto the bird table and then it got onto the windowsill and it went up and down, up and down, trying to find a way in. It scrabbled up on the glass trying to find a way through.'

Both my parents were busy replying to the many messages of sympathy they had received, including one from Peter Cooper, who had won my father's respect.

'No, Cooper must be written to. He might take offence.'

On Sunday morning I found my father writing a long letter to Edward and Michiko in Bangkok, using an economy blue airmail form.

'It is good and kind of you both to cable back so promptly with your sympathy,' he began and went on to write of Ben's 'golden years of solid achievement' in the hotel and advertising trades. 'A beloved son, I will say no more.'

His letter ended with a short paragraph about what my father obliquely described as 'family matters'. 'These are being dealt with by Mr Sweet and you will hear from him later on. In the meantime I will, later this month, let you know roughly how matters stand.'

Certain people were quicker to offer their sympathy than others and my father kept remembering people who had so far failed to do so. 'Look here, we've heard nothing from Colonel Cocky.'

As so often before, my parents stayed in separate places when they came to London the following day. My mother stayed with Tim and me in the studio. My father stayed at Richard's house.

On Monday afternoon, we all met at the Brompton Oratory for the arrival of the two coffins. Two friends of Susi were present, the Yorkshire lady and a skinny fashion model named Pauline, but no relations.

After the short service conducted by the same priest who had been preparing Ben and Susi for marriage, Tim escorted Pauline to the back of the church to show her a mural by a famous pre-Raphaelite painter, a public statement that as far as he was concerned there were other things in life besides this particular family tragedy.

That night there was a meal at Richard's house. The tragedy had not had the effect of uniting the family. On the contrary, the divisions were heightened and sharp looks were exchanged.

During the course of the evening, it was suddenly remembered that Ben's old housemaster – a man named Trinder – might not know of the tragedy or of the following day's service, and Richard was sent to telephone him. As he climbed the narrow stairs he suddenly turned back, glared at me and without a smile told me not to listen on the extension.

My father remained buoyant, repeatedly referring to Ben as his 'golden boy'. Of the priest who would also be conducting the next day's requiem, he said: 'I don't think he would get on very well in Quaker circles. He was smelling very heavily of whisky at five o'clock in the afternoon.'

There was also some talk about a bachelor friend of Ben's called Crispin Gray who that morning had published a glowing tribute to my younger brother in *The Times*. My father was planning to express his gratitude by sending him a case of claret.

'I'm assuming he's a young married man with children who'll be very pleased to have six dinner parties covered.'

*

The following morning, my father stood alone on the steps of the Brompton Oratory welcoming mourners as they arrived for the Requiem. This was an odd thing to do and my mother did not stand beside him. I slipped past without pausing and inside was delighted to find Aunt Peg, who had arrived overnight, waiting to embrace me in front of several hundred people, some of whom were sobbing.

After the service, I lingered on the steps as the coffins were placed in their hearses.

'Go and sit in the car,' ordered Richard. I meekly did so and when the limousine pulled away I saw Crispin Gray – in an orange suit – waving enthusiastically from the pavement.

At the burial service in Putney Cemetery, Richard told me to do up the buttons of my overcoat and my mother surprised me by suddenly putting her arm round a pretty woman I learnt later was Susi's mother. My brother and his fiancée were buried in the same grave. I still did not cry because I still could not believe they were dead.

*

After the funeral, Tim's studio was put to social use. A lunch of cold meats was served. White wine flowed. The Yorkshire lady – the only outsider – harangued my mother about something. A remote cousin of my father – a socialist, my father had often said – helped himself to more wine and lit a pipe.

At the end of the meal, I talked to the woman I now knew was Susi's mother.

'She was a wonderful person,' I said.

'Well, I think so too,' she replied. 'But I'm biased.'

The only people missing – apart from my grandmother – were Michiko and Edward. My father had strongly advised them not to make the trip – and they had accepted his advice. Michiko was anyhow now six months pregnant.

A long letter from Edward was already on its way to me, however, in which he offered his sympathy and recalled the intimacy that he, Ben and I had shared during our early childhood. The letter continued on a sterner note with a reference to the bank for which Edward had been working for six years – 'I am gradually assuming additional responsibilities here' – and finally posed the question, 'Do you think all this will affect Father's depressing plan of moving to the Isle of Man?'

19

A few days after the requiem, I was driven north by Jack Pratt. He was going fishing in Scotland and would drop me off in Cumberland on the way. Like several of those most closely involved, Jack seemed to have taken the tragedy in his stride – in the sense of not being down trodden about it.

He declared that there was a 'very strange smell' about the whole affair and subscribed to my tiny lingering suspicions that it was still a hoax by saying that he was absolutely sure that we would eventually meet Ben again.

My aunt's cottage was in worse disorder than before – and there was a much worse smell of cats. Aunt Peg's constant battle to get from one part of the cottage to another – and get the better of the cats – created a continual sense of drama.

'It was while I was working at the sink and the meat was lying out that I was so worried,' she said in a grave, hesitant tone few actresses could have attempted.

When she talked of Ben she sounded more jubilant.

'He was your creation,' she suddenly declared. 'You brought him out. He was your discovery.'

The following day we were playing chess as usual when Tim arrived unexpectedly.

'Who's winning?' he asked.

'Nobody's winning yet,' said Peg. 'It's too early.'

The cats annoyed Tim, who was used to staying in comfortable houses with well-trained pets.

'I'm quite willing to go out and strangle that cat now,' he said.

My aunt heard the remark and replied, after several minutes' silence, 'I'm not going to have him killed. He's a lovely cat.'

*

Tim and I drove south, stopped at Liverpool and took a plane to the Isle of Man. This was pure curiosity on our part. We wanted to see what sort of folly our father was committing.

'I haven't been on a plane for three weeks,' boasted Tim as we boarded the tiny aircraft. 'You see,' he added when we were airborne, 'Nothing to worry about really.'

Then his attention was caught by a plump stewardess. 'Would I like to take her on the slow boat to China!' he declared.

On the island Tim hired a car and we drove around my father's intended homeland, inspected the tiny cottage that awaited him and booked in for the night at a seafront hotel in Douglas.

Here Tim announced that he would be visiting the local casino later. 'I'm going to play some blackjack,' he said adjusting his tie.

Over supper in a Chinese restaurant we talked about Ben. Tim described in detail the identification of the bodies and even sketched on a napkin the profile our brother had presented on the mortuary slab.

Not for the first time, he spoke disparagingly about the relationship between Ben and Susi and blamed himself for being out of England during the early stages of the friendship.

'If I'd known they were having an affair, I'd have made absolutely certain they didn't marry,' he said. 'Their wedding would have been an absolute fiasco. The funeral only went well because it was brilliantly organised by Richard.'

We touched lightly on Edward.

'Edward had much hairier arms than you or I,' said Tim. 'It's probably the East, they sweat a lot out there.'

Early the following morning, I heard Tim's radio alarm clock in the next room, as my much-travelled brother kept abreast of the day's news from far beyond the Isle of Man.

20

The threads of my life remained woven with Ben's. I hung up his pictures around the flat. I used his alarm clocks. I went to his hairdresser. I wore his clothes – including the cuff-links which the police had retrieved – and saw his friends.

By a cruel irony, I only got to meet many of Ben's friends because he was dead. It was impossible to go out without an encounter with someone who knew Ben. I nursed the wound his death had inflicted on me and made the most of it.

'Did Ben want to die?' people asked and their grief kept the mystery fresh in my mind.

Almost every day, a letter arrived from Mr Blunt. These were full of requests for the sort of favours Ben must have provided. His current object in life was to get his wardrobe sufficiently in order that he could obtain a residential tutoring post. He also required a suitcase in which to place his new clothes – and so on. He asked often for me to visit him at Oxford where he was now in the alcoholic unit of a lunatic asylum.

When I accepted this invitation, he was overjoyed – and I was also excited to see this remarkable surviving friend of my brother's. I found him wearing the same tweed jacket he had on when I first met him and a pair of trousers that had once belonged to Ben. A sprig of heather protruded from his buttonhole.

Over lunch in the hospital canteen, Blunt told me of his first meeting with Ben. 'I was in Yates's wine bar. Talking to Mrs Clark. When Jack and Ben came in and sat opposite, Mrs Clark said, "Don't look now but those two are watching you. They're very interested in you."'

More letters followed this meeting and then a letter which began in Blunt's usual conversational style but ended with him saying that he would not be writing again, he was severing all his connections with the past and any letter I might send him would be returned 'unopened, unread and unwanted'.

I had also seen a bit of the Yorkshire lady. She was insatiably hospitable and had continued giving parties in the Chelsea Green flat which had been Ben's last home. She had succeeded in recruiting into her circle not only Jack Pratt – 'He's weird, isn't he? I just find him incredibly weird' – but also the priest who had conducted the Requiem. She sniffed out social occasions everywhere and on hearing that Tim was soon to leave London asked if he was going to give a farewell party for himself. She had opinions, too, about the Isle of Man. 'Everyone drinks like a fish there,' she said.

Unlike many of Ben's friends, the Yorkshire lady did not dwell on past events but steamed ahead indefatigably – and eventually out of my life.

This was not the case with Pauline, the skinny model whom Tim had briefly befriended at the Brompton Oratory. When I visited Pauline at her flat she talked bitterly about the affair and especially about Susi, whom she had apparently known for several years.

'They were hopeless together,' she said. 'I tried to stop it but could do nothing. She was making Ben into something he didn't want to be . . . That was half the attraction. But she was brave and strong. You had to admire that girl for what she did for herself. She once bought a handbag for a thousand pounds . . . She was desperately insecure . . . She was terribly frightened of your parents . . . She was terrified of meeting them . . .'

This sad monologue continued until I left Pauline framed in the doorway of her flat, a sad and lonely figure bereft of her closest friend. Suddenly her thoughts turned briefly to my eldest brother.

'Richard is a completely foreign body to me. I mean, what produced him?'

*

I had not seen much of Richard, who was busy selling his house and planning his move to a bigger one, but I saw and heard a lot of Tim, who was thumping across the ceiling all the time he was in London. Tim was quite domesticated in his own way, but his studio had few facilities of its own and he was dependent on the flat's kitchen and bathroom. I would often hear the rattle of a kettle lid or find him washing up, or hear him whistling wearily in a way which reminded me of my mother.

Sometimes he would enter my room and find me puffing at a cigarette as I tried to work up the inspiration to begin typing.

'Smoking at this hour!' he tut-tutted.

'I'm trying to relax, Tim,' I replied. 'You're just fluttering about like a butterfly.'

'I've lost the laundry list.'

During the next few weeks, Tim's flurry of activity increased – the studio filled with packing cases, bundles of stretchers, paint-boxes and other equipment – as he prepared to leave for America where he had several commissions waiting and the promise of a one-man show later in the summer.

Impatient though he was to get away, Tim still turned over in his mind the tragic affair of Ben and Susi and by the time of his departure seemed, like me, to have become aware of some vague undefined mystery about the glamorous young woman who had so nearly become our sister-in-law.

'Richard and I were saying last night that she would probably have ended up in prison or a loony bin,' he said on the last morning. 'Ben was either very stupid. Or mad. He regarded it all as a joke.'

Then he began to lug his cases downstairs, some of which were labelled 'BOAC cargo'.

'Make me a Bovril sandwich quickly,' he commanded. 'Liz Ashley's driving me to the airport in half an hour.'

21

Since Ben's death, television had been more or less banned from my father's house – 'We've had nothing but the News for five weeks,' said my mother – and the tragedy was constantly referred to.

'I may be the next to go,' said my father. 'Taken straight off. And not necessarily to Heaven either.'

There was still talk about the Requiem, about the presence in the congregation of a duke and also of some people my father described as 'upper-class Jews'.

My mother talked about the Yorkshire lady who gate-crashed the family party after the service.

'She rather rode over you and made you feel small.'

For Susi herself there were only the faintest rumbles of disapproval.

'Was she a rogue?' my father asked half-jokingly, but the only fault he could find with her was that she was a Catholic.

'Grandpapa would simply have said, "My great-grandson has been playing around with Catholics." Aunt Dot made it quite clear to me that if I married a Catholic, I wasn't going to see much in the way of a present from her.'

'Aunt Dot wasn't like that at all,' protested my mother.

'She didn't like Catholics. Terrible business.'

My mother pointed out that some of my father's closest acquaintances were Catholic, but my father stuck to his guns.

'I don't mind! I dare say I've slept with a few – but don't marry 'em!'

When my mother was out of the room, he returned to the subject. 'Your mother doesn't like Catholics. Never has. Granny loathes them!'

Suddenly Catholics had joined those groups he hated. Or pretended to hate. It was getting increasingly difficult to tell what he really felt.

'I don't want any more flashy people, foreigners, or any people of that sort, coming into this family,' he said later in the weekend. 'For heaven's sake, let's have some hundred percenters.'

On the whole my mother was getting back to her own life, the garden, even some fishing, while my father raked through the embers of Ben's life, hoping to find some glowing twig. He replied at length to everyone who had written offering sympathy and to thank all those who had sent flowers. In some cases he seemed to have entered into a correspondence.

To Ben's employers, my father had written enclosing his son's company pass. The staff manager had duly acknowledged this and politely enquired if he could assist in any way. My father had replied by return post stating that Ben had left his affairs in 'apple pie order'.

It was more shocking to learn that in his grief my father had telephoned the local Wiltshire paper and told a reporter not only about the crash but also about how much money my brother had left. During the weekend, my father took me aside and sheepishly showed me the article which had resulted, muttering as he did so that my mother was 'not pleased'.

The article faithfully charted my brother's career as seen by my father – 'He worked as a kitchen porter at the Dorchester Hotel before deciding to go into advertising. He started as a clerk but soon became a top copywriter whose work was attracting considerable attention.' There was no mention at all of Ben's pictures.

It was a relief when my father eventually turned to other topics. Principal among these was his move to the Isle of Man. Ben's death had had no effect on these plans, nor had the recent return of a Conservative government. In fact he had now begun to show the house to prospective purchasers, exhausting my mother afterwards with comments and speculations.

'Really, I don't think I've ever had such an unpleasant female visitor as the woman who came round today. I think she made a psychological mistake bringing four small children. I really cannot believe that that woman was in such a state financially that she couldn't afford to have someone look after them for a few hours.'

He returned to this subject a few hours later. 'That woman

was quite obviously Left-Wing. She was very frosty when I said the Conservatives meet here.'

His grief had not dislodged his other favourite topics. Nor had the tragedy changed my parents' characters in any way. When I suggested that they should seize this opportunity to visit Edward and Michiko in Bangkok my mother said flatly, 'I doubt our affording that,' and I could see there was no point in pursuing this.

The topic of Ben was never far away – and was tackled on many levels.

'Where was Ben's local?' asked my father, seeking a fresh angle on Ben's London life.

My father had already decided to commemorate his youngest son's life in various ways. He had persuaded Tim to paint a portrait of Ben from a photograph and he was much involved in a plan to plant two copper beeches at the spot where the young lovers had died.

22

My life in London was soon complicated by Mr Blunt's reappearance. Ben's old friend had not succeeded in cutting his links with the past and indeed was desperate for help, encouragement and material support. He had left Oxford and was back at the mercy of the London streets. He telephoned me frequently. I met him in pubs, on park benches and in churches – just as my brother had done.

Our meetings sometimes began with long silences. When he was not drunk he spoke in a broken, soft voice of unusual pernicketiness.

One morning I got a call from the Samaritans on his behalf.

'He's been a client of ours for some time,' said the lady. 'He does seem very, very low, almost at the end.'

All Blunt needed was a drink, and after an hour in a Chelsea pub I left him sipping a mixture of sherry and tomato juice – a session which, I learnt later, ended with him being arrested drunk and disorderly.

It was soon after this incident that I took Blunt to see Susi's old friend Pauline. For some reason or another, Pauline seemed attracted to Blunt and wanted to help him, or perhaps to cling onto him because for her too he represented a last surviving part of Ben and Susi's world.

Blunt seemed at ease in Pauline's flat and Pauline seemed prepared to take him under her wing.

'For six months,' she told him. 'You need a baby-sitter.'

It was arranged that Blunt should move into her flat – and it was there that I left him. Both he and Pauline were drinking plain tomato juice and Blunt was telling her how Mickey Mouse was invented.

'As simple as that! Touché,' said Pauline when he had finished.

She had suddenly become strangely possessive of the old man and pushed me towards the door. On the doorstep she managed one parting shot only.

'Your father's gone potty, hasn't he? He's sent me a round-the-bend letter saying, "I want to clear my son's name."'

23

There was some truth in Pauline's remark. My father had certainly changed his tune since the inquest. Though it was now the summer, his mind remained firmly focused on the tragic event of early April. He was obsessed with the details of the accident and determined to prove that Ben had not been driving the car at the time. To everyone he could think of, he now wrote officiously, 'There is no evidence whatsoever that my son was driving but very strong evidence indeed that the driver's seat was occupied by his fiancée.'

He was even considering placing an advertisement in the local Buckinghamshire newspaper to see if any new witness might emerge who could support his claim. For Susi herself and her way of life, he now had nothing but contempt, though after reading the pathologist's report he admitted ruefully, 'The poor brute really paid for it in the last minute and a half of her life.'

*

In spite of my father's terrible new obsession and his increasing involvement in the technicalities of his move to the Isle of Man, my Wiltshire weekends that summer followed the pattern established years earlier. When I telephoned announcing a visit, I was often answered with my father's warning that he would not meet any train arriving after 9 p.m. On arrival at the house, my father would identify the room I was to occupy by referring to its last occupant.

'You're in Mr Sweet's room,' he said one weekend.

Mr Sweet, the family accountant, had recently stayed at the house to work on the administration of Ben's estate and had been given an inferior back bedroom.

Another weekend, I was assigned the room my grandmother had occupied. Though cleared of her possessions, a faint smell lingered which reminded me of her occupancy. There were as yet no signs that the house was to be disbanded, though my mother worked harder than usual in the garden so that it should look its best to prospective purchasers. My father mowed the lawns – 'dead easy', Ben had once remarked – and my mother still protested at his habit of throwing the clippings behind a hedge or over a wall.

'I was gardening very late last night,' said my mother one morning, 'about eight o'clock – and Daddy's mouldy grass was stinking. Also I was being bitten by midges which I'm sure were coming out of the grass.'

Though busier than usual, my father still had time to brood. I would often find him in his chair beside the telephone, gazing at his hands, still looking as if he was trying to read his own palms or perhaps now searching for signs of rheumatism.

'What are you doing?'

'I'm looking at the hands of a very, very stupid man.'

Another time I found him standing on the staircase, head cocked.

'Do you hear a noise going on now? Sort of pipes? Listen.'

'I can't hear anything.'

'Well I can. It's a noise of water running through the house.'

Sooner or later, I would be subjected to a private talk in his study: 'Come in and close the door.'

This was never a dialogue in which my advice or opinions were sought but always a monologue following the same pattern. It would start with little titbits – 'What crowing there would be in the Catholic belfries if Tim married Liz Ashley.' Then would come the further decline of Barbara Barton – 'She is likely to be confined in St Saviour's'; his own war record – 'No one can say that I was either a bad soldier or a good soldier because I had no active service'; his will and Richard's privileged position in it – 'Quite naturally, as eldest son, in addition to the extra money I've already given him'; Great Aunt Amy's will – 'D'you want a copy? I'm getting several'; and so on and so forth until suddenly the throat would be cleared and the tone become more rigid. 'Now the question is this, William,' he would say and launch into his current major obsession.

Again and again that summer, my father tried to blame Ben's death on the girl he had nearly married. His hostility now extended to the whole of Susi's social circle and included in its web not only the harmless Yorkshire lady – 'She is known to every police division in London' – but most of the other residents of Chelsea.

After thoroughly airing this subject, it was a relief when he turned to other topics. He now mocked the family into which he himself had married with increasing gusto, singling out for attack my mother's great-grandfather, who had been a general in the Indian Army: 'Your great-great-grandfather had a very serious attack of what used to be called gum. He was in a Bangalore dispensary for a very long time and it was a most disgraceful matter.'

For me, too, there was plenty of teasing and mockery but he never questioned me about my work – I was now trying to become a freelance journalist – or asked me about my marriage plans.

'Could you get a salaried job within a month?' he asked suddenly. When I replied with a firm negative, he merely smiled complacently.

Since Ben's death, he had become oddly indulgent to me.

'That's it!' he suddenly exclaimed one meal time. 'The defrocked minister! I've been trying to place him for a long time. When were you chucked out of Selwyn, old boy?'

If I said something which annoyed him, he now over-reacted wildly.

'You're going to be sent to a mental hospital if you make remarks like that. And shaken till you're absolutely breathless.'

This line of conversation often culminated in an unsavoury description of physical punishment in store for me.

'You know what Admiral Towpath would do with you if you were on his ship? Your buttocks would soon be running with blood! Oh, William!' his voice rose to an excited crescendo, 'The rope's end!'

Much of the time he now spoke to me in a strange string of self-conscious clichés or other arch utterances. 'You'd better go upstairs and rest,' 'Put self last,' and 'Get that out of that silly head of yours.' He was a little calmer when he discussed my social life and vigorous when he tried to steer me away from the Chelsea world of which he now held such a low opinion.

'I'd like to see you going out to dinner at least twice a week with established people. Wearing your dinner-jacket.'

This garment remained a sacred object. My father's was thirty-five years old. He had worn it on the night he first met my mother and it was still going strong. Mine had been made when I was twenty. My father had teased me about how little I had used it but after my younger brother's death had written me a fearsome postcard, 'On no account dispose of Ben's dinner-jacket.'

His only real concern seemed to be that I should be able to pay my income tax, and hardly a weekend passed without some reference to my finances. One breakfast time he cleared his throat and said, 'Now about your bankruptcy proceedings . . .'

*

My mother sat through these discussions, these wranglings about Ben and jokes about her great-grandfather, without reacting. Her mind remained firmly focused on domestic matters.

'I'm worried about the hens,' she said one weekend. 'My

five old ladies have practically stopped laying. They're laying one or two a day, which isn't enough.'

Another time it was the dogs that concerned her.

'Gilda is definitely on heat,' she announced. 'She spilt in my bed, naughty gal. Still she may peter out. Oh, it is a curse having mixed sexes in one house. I don't know why I did it,' she added after locking up the old dog in a room at the back of the house.

At the end of each day, my mother seemed increasingly tired and unable to cope. 'I want to lie my head down on my pillow and sleep', she said one evening immediately after supper, inspiring another of my father's rather grim, sketchy, oblique lectures on his wife's health.

*

From time to time that summer my parents' attention was diverted to other matters. Ben's death had been followed by happier family events. In June or July, Sally gave birth to another girl, while in Bangkok there was a more dramatic delivery. Michiko gave birth to a boy who was given names which gave no clue to his half-Japanese background. Toby John Philip were the names my brother chose. Letters and cards from Edward and Michiko were brief and to the point, their way of life an unknown quantity though a postcard showing the block of flats they lived in failed to impress my father.

'What a ghastly place,' he said. 'Looks like a bloody prison!'

My mother remained focused on the dogs. 'Oh, by the way, Gilda gave Tommy a real snarl this morning. Which usually means shop's shut.'

There were also visitors. Among these were my father's old friend Bobbie. I missed this event but learnt about it in a letter from my mother. 'We were shocked by her manner on the first night,' she wrote. 'I thought she was either tight or had had a stroke but she miraculously recovered in the night and became nicer and she stayed three days.'

A more distinguished guest had been Crispin Gray, author of the tribute to Ben which had appeared in *The Times*. Again I missed the visit – I saw Crispin occasionally in London – but my mother told me about it later.

'He was simply charming. He walked round the garden in the rain with Father. I asked him to lunch but he couldn't stay because he was going to a concert in Bath.'

Later she referred to him again.

'Crispin Gray had bare feet and sandals with a coloured shirt. In other words, William, you look too towny.'

My father also pondered over the visit and twice remarked, 'I got the impression Crispin Gray didn't like me.'

*

Some of my visits coincided with those of Richard. His presence shook things up a little, bringing with him the efficient, modern methods of the company for which he worked. He now tried to handle my father in a robust way and interrupt his more monotonous monologues.

'Well perhaps I have different values to you', 'Well then you've got nothing to worry about', 'I'm afraid I don't understand what you're on about,' and other brusque remarks along these lines were designed to steer my father into slightly more orthodox conversations.

Soon my father was talking about golf – 'When did you meet your Waterloo? I reckon Miller's a shocking golfer myself' – then about the drains under the house that Richard was in the process of buying off the Brompton Road. From time to time Richard tried to get my mother to join in the conversation or at least to join the circle.

'Can't,' said my mother, her hands full of mending and sewing. Sooner or later, my father would get the better of his eldest son and Richard would collapse deflated.

'I feel so tired I really am quite worried about myself. I'm so tired I think I'm going to bed. I'm mentally and physically tired.'

He retreated to the kitchen where to emphasise his fatigue he now made himself a mug of cocoa.

'Of course you'll make yourself podgy drinking that stuff,' said my father, who had followed him through the house.

'I shall be up in my room, Father, writing a letter to my wife. I'll come down and say goodnight to you before I go to bed.'

This was a tactic to try and prevent my father entering his bedroom and taking advantage of his state of undress. My father often did this, sometimes even turning the light on and waking a son up, then putting the knife in – 'Why are you casual and unbusinesslike?' – or perhaps barging in as one was relaxing over a cigarette – 'You'll only do your health harm by constant smoking.'

He still confined himself to the one solitary cigarette a day, last thing at night, and a cigar once or twice a week, leaving the sodden ends in a bathroom basin. He did not go in for ashtrays, perhaps through some puritan refusal to plan his pleasures.

*

Most weekends people came to view the house. My father enjoyed showing them round, chatting with them and patronising them, and did not seem in the least downcast when a prospective purchaser dropped out.

'This house will sell,' he told me confidently. 'This is one of the finest properties round Bath.'

To potential purchasers he spoke of his interest in lawns and in particular his miniature golf course. 'I've got these three holes,' he explained. 'I do the maintenance myself. Green keeping, that's my hobby.'

He sometimes spoke of his family's history – 'We've been Quaker since 1722. I've never thought of changing' – and even of the tragedy that had recently afflicted the family. 'It's yours,' he said, pressing Ben's re-printed *Times* obituary into the hands of a mystified visitor.

He also talked about his own plans to move to the Isle of Man. 'I've already got my own property there,' he said loftily.

Afterwards he would talk about these people at length. One man he described as 'a typical film type with an excessively high colour'. Another man, managing director of a Bristol firm, 'may be the man who built up the business'.

Disregarding the delay in selling the house, my father pressed ahead with the preparation of his Isle of Man cottage.

'I have ordered an outer front door and an inner window to our sitting room,' he told me in a letter.

Already he had opened two different bank accounts on the island, and the Isle of Man Bank, for which he was developing an unholy respect, featured frequently in his conversations.

There were still a few calm moments. Sometimes I would be able to stop my father's flow and turn on the television – and with luck get him interested in a programme, reaching for his gold-framed circular spectacles, which he rarely wore and which he clipped onto his face with some palaver. Wearing these he looked formidably concentrated, and if the programme interested him enough all outside worries and enthusiasms were temporarily excluded.

First thing in the morning he was also calm, subdued by sleep, and his brain rested. One morning I heard my mother talking to him in his bedroom as gently as a nurse and him replying in feeble tones as if semi-senile.

'You haven't used your pot.'

'Have. 'Fraid so. Yes.'

Once up and dressed in his uncomfortable clothing, he was again on the rampage, striding into whatever room I was in, giving orders – 'Open the curtains please, natural light.' Or even more vigorously showing off in the kitchen by tap-dancing for the benefit of the daily woman. He was not quite as good as in the old days and once he missed his footing.

'Oh my God, I nearly went down on my back!'

After breakfast, he became more aggressive, sometimes telephoning the station to find out the time of the train on which I should return to London the next day. Calls to his various advisors would follow. To Mr Trump, Mr Midwinter and the others had now been added a new name, Mr Quayle of the Isle of Man Bank, and to this key new acquaintance my father spoke with appropriate reverence several times a week.

My father still went to church – though when he got there he played little part in the service, singing only the opening line of each hymn or canticle after which his lips remained as compressed as they would at a Quaker Meeting. He was much more interested in the practical and financial side of church life and that summer expressed suspicion about a new appeal for vicarage repairs.

'I'm wondering if this isn't a concealed way of trying to get the vicar a capital sum.'

*

Though my parents hoped soon to leave the house for good, they did not break their habit of going away on separate summer holidays. My mother went north to visit my grandmother, now in her ninety-second year – 'Sometimes she's very muddled. Sometimes she's much straighter' – and also to stay with Aunt Peg, and to walk and fish.

My father headed East on a tour of golf courses. Bridlington, Frinton and Felixstowe. 'I shall simply drink beer and play golf,' he explained, adding, 'You know, the ordinary city clerk is getting a very poor return for his money by going to Devon or Cornwall. He'd get a much better deal on the Norfolk coast.'

I was present on the eve of my mother's departure and I noticed her calmness and quietness as she moved around the house making preparations for the long solitary car journey north.

'Next week we will both be away,' my father told me in a semi-official manner. 'The house will be closed and the garden patrolled.'

24

The relationship between Mr Blunt and Pauline the model had not worked out.

'Your friend,' she soon screamed hysterically at me down the telephone, 'has stolen a hundred pounds from me!'

This call was followed by a much calmer one from the Chelsea police. 'Have you any idea,' asked a detective, 'how we could get in touch with Mr Blunt?'

I did not offer any suggestions, and in fact I never saw Blunt again. 'I should imagine he's pretty adept at disappearing without trace,' said Crispin Gray when I informed him of this latest development in the aftermath of Ben's death.

Meanwhile, my peaceful domestic life had been partly disrupted by Tim's return from New York. From the floor below I would hear his footsteps as he hurried to answer the telephone, which rang continuously now he was home. In the evenings these footsteps would merge with the tread of other feet and often the tip-tap of high heels.

Several times a day, Tim would descend to the flat and make himself a snack, a cup of coffee, munch an apple or express mild irritation with the sounds that came from my room.

'Is it necessary to make such a noise with your typewriter? Bang! Bang! Bang! Bang!'

I would often return to the flat to find Tim rustling about, humming a little tune, sneezing or running himself a bath. In the morning I would hear his joints creaking as he made his breakfast, the clunk of his bowl on the work surface, the rustle of a cereal packet and the scrape of a saucepan on the hob. Sometimes he would enter the room and give me a plate containing half a scrambled egg.

Tim's main interest beside painting was social life. He was attracted to and fitted effortlessly into the mainstream. Though acquainted with some of his more fashionable contemporaries, such as the tailor living downstairs, he preferred a more sedate and respectable life and one night that summer spoke in disparaging terms of a 'wife-swapping party' he had found himself at in Hampstead. Tim's circle and the rackety, colourful gang that had engulfed Ben hardly overlapped, and I sometimes got the impression that Tim regarded Ben's demise as an inevitable consequence of straying too far outside the ordered world.

He did not share my exalted opinion of Ben's talents as an artist – and he had not adapted his opinion because of the

tragedy. Tim had an instinctive sense of who was really significant – and this did not include many of the practitioners or
collectors of Modern Art. My friends did not interest him –
and he even expressed relief that Peter Cooper had left England
again. 'I had virtually no time at all for him', he said. 'I think
he was a boring little man.' Tim's heroes were the semi-phil-
istine owners of stately homes: he was extremely popular
among them and their offspring. Now in his early thirties but
still unmarried, he was a beloved figure in these circles, where
few artists roamed, and within a few days of his return to
England that summer was able to boast that his diary was
completely full. The subtle charm which he used so successfully
on my mother had bowled over many mightier figures. Letters
in the confident handwriting of these people often filled his
ground floor pigeonhole, whether he was in England or not.

In spite of his busy life, Tim always found time to gossip
about his friends and he would sometimes enter the flat at
the end of the evening, slightly drunk, suit crinkled and happy
to talk about what he had done.

What Tim thought of my own struggle towards freelance
writing I could not tell, but one day that summer he uttered
a solemn warning. 'You mustn't compare yourself with me.
I've been terribly lucky.'

He would also sometimes venture a mild criticism of my
appearance. 'William, you've had rather an unsuccessful shave.
It's a complete mess. You've shaved parts. You've cut yourself.
Are you trying to grow a beard?'

*

At the height of the summer, life in the flat was further
disturbed by the presence of Richard. My eldest brother had
now sold the house on Campden Hill and his new home was

not yet ready. Sally and the children were in Sussex. Richard had seized the opportunity to return to the world of his younger brothers.

'What a nice flat this is,' he said, moving in with several smart suitcases, a bag of golf clubs and other items for which there was not enough space in the small back room. Soon a neat row of well-polished winklepickers, all fitted with wooden shoe-trees, appeared in the passage outside my room, while Richard himself, clad in a kimono, moved around the small kitchen like an athlete, making a hot milk drink for himself and Tim.

'You must get very cold here in the winter,' he said.

The following morning, I heard my eldest brother whistling on the lavatory and tearing paper cheerfully.

'Make me a cup of coffee,' he called.

He then brushed his hair vigorously and set off for his office, carrying two briefcases. I listened as his car roared away up the street. Five minutes later, I heard the roar again. He had forgotten his keys to the flat.

*

Richard's spell of independence was brief. At the end of the summer he moved into his new home off the Brompton Road, and when I telephoned him there soon afterwards he sounded as sluggish as ever.

'You've interrupted me in the middle of lunch,' he said. 'Sally is going to go and have a sleep.'

This unpromising beginning was followed by an invitation to tea that afternoon. The atmosphere of their former home had now been stretched over five floors, and the same dainty furniture, coffee table with brass-hinged flaps, photos in silver frames and leather club fender occupied the sunny first-floor drawing room.

'Let me take your coat.'

Whatever Sally and Richard's feelings were about their new house, they were not revealing them, and as far as I knew no house-warming celebrations were planned.

Tea was served in the basement dining room.

'I feel I must have a rest,' said Richard. 'I feel exhausted.'

My efforts to start a conversation were met with grunts, and it was only after a supreme effort that Richard began to talk about Tim, whom he had got to know better during the spell under his roof.

'I must say Tim seems to be surrounded by gay young people,' he said.

'Gay?' I said.

'Not in The Boys In The Band sense,' he added hastily.

We then moved two floors up to the drawing room where we were joined by a girl friend of Sally's, who was also seeing the new house for the first time.

At one moment the girl's gaze fell upon a snapshot of Susi which lay on the mantelpiece.

'That was a girl who was killed in a car crash,' Sally explained. 'She was engaged to Richard's brother.'

Finally, my eldest brother stood on his new doorstep with me and volunteered, 'I'm off to Belgium on Tuesday for two days, I'm happy to say. To visit our laboratories.'

25

My father's house at last found a purchaser. A certain Dr Gummer agreed to pay four times what my father had paid for the place sixteen years earlier.

When I visited the house for the last time I found it transformed. The surviving dogs had already gone. Aunt Peg had agreed to harbour them during the move and had undertaken to bring them with her to the Isle of Man at Christmas. Every piece of furniture in the house now carried an eye-catching coloured label.

The cottage would have room for only a few essentials. A lot was to go into store on the island, standing by in the event of my father buying a larger house. A great deal had already been distributed to my surviving brothers and carried a label to indicate its destiny.

Richard and Sally's items – the grandfather clock, various chairs and chests of drawers – were marked in red. Those marked in blue had been selected by Tim as suitable for his studio, while those marked in yellow were to be put in store for Edward and Michiko in case they should ever establish a home in England. Though I was happy to accept some books and other sundry items, I had snootily declined to participate in the share-out of the larger pieces, with so many of which I had only gloomy associations.

'Hurry up and get married,' urged my mother, suggesting that I might soon regret this decision.

A certain number of fixtures and fittings and garden equipment would be acquired by the new owner of the house, Dr Gummer, and I found my father on the telephone to the estate agent discussing the pricing of these items.

'A new, relatively new, gas fire in my study – two pounds? Ought we to charge more? There is local demand for one lawn roller. What are they worth? Four pounds each? Now the thing is this . . .'

With a curious absence of sentimentality, my father now seemed willing to fling away possessions he had known since childhood. Handing me a big *History of Lancashire*, all he said was 'We've got no room for that sort of thing.'

However, he followed this gift with a coarse jibe.

'You're taking it because you're likely to be very hard up in the future. You're taking it to flog it!'

And as I walked off with the volume he shouted after me, 'Let me see you carrying the book properly! Without mutilating its pages!'

In the midst of this confusion my father still had time to pause and ponder over the portrait of himself which had been done during his final year at the Board of Trade. This had been accepted by Richard and carried the appropriate red label.

'That portrait is a work of art,' he said, 'It shows a picture of an over-worked senior civil servant.'

During these final days, my father also found time to write a long letter to Edward and Michiko which began with a benevolent reference to their baby son – more jocularly described to his other grandchildren as 'Aunt Meekoko's boy, Cousin Toby' – and continued with a harmless reference to myself and my hairstyle: 'William here this weekend looking like a hooded raven, so he could not be taken to church.' The letter ended on a more practical note. 'Mother is listing all the silver which will be sent over to the Isle of Man Bank.'

This clearing-up process reminded my mother of the much bigger sorting-out she had been involved with in the early years of her marriage when my father's old family home on the outskirts of Lancaster had been disbanded.

'When we turned out Parkfield,' she began, 'we found ottomans packed tight with letters. We found drawers full of broken china. We also found rather nice things, like the dolls' dinner service. We put a lot of stuff in a sale and it didn't sell.'

My mother was happiest when deciding which plants she was going to take with her.

'I'm going to take lots of primulas in little plastic pots. I'm also going to take the campanula that runs down the steps because I'm so fond of him.'

My father was now in the process of severing most of his links with the past, changing his investments into government stock and giving up his remaining positions.

'For revenue reasons,' he explained to the local vicar and policeman, 'I am going to reside overseas.'

'I have resigned from the Reform Club,' he informed me in one of his letters. 'When I am a Manxman, I hope rejoining can be considered. Until then it is simply not worth it.'

Even at this late hour, my father still sought to justify the great decision he had made. 'The cost of living has gone up barbarously,' he said.

My father had also been trying to establish a few social contacts on the Isle of Man – and had been cultivating the old bachelor named Parker who lived in the next parish and happened to own a holiday cottage on the island. My father had never shown interest in this man before – indeed had more than once described him as 'a mouldy old thing' – but now he was on the telephone to him twice a day, buttering him up, inviting him to play golf and consulting him about Manx affairs.

'Look here, are you doing anything tonight? We're very much on our own here.'

Finally, my father had an unexpected announcement. 'I'm

going to have the central heating on,' he said. 'I'm not going to risk having a cold here next week.'

*

At the end of November my parents set off in convoy – my mother in the Morris Minor, my father in the Rover, for the first lap of their journey to the Isle of Man. That evening, my father telephoned me from a small hotel near Liverpool where they were spending the night before boarding an early morning steamer. He sounded over-excited and pleased with himself.

'Are you sad to be leaving England?' I asked.

'No, I'm greatly relieved that this mountain of responsibility has been taken off my shoulders.'

'How's Mummy?'

'She's upstairs. Very tired.'

The following morning, my mother and father, aged sixty and sixty-three respectively, sailed away to their uncertain future on board a vessel of the Isle of Man Steam Packet Company.

PART TWO

1

'Press button A, please, Isle of Man.'

The telephone had not been installed at the cottage, and my parents were obliged to go to the kiosk at the end of the lane. My mother was trying to persuade me to start my Christmas visit a day earlier so that Aunt Peg and I could be met off the same boat.

'You can't come on Tuesday? Peg is bringing the dogs, that's the whole point.'

When I eventually reached the cottage, I found Aunt Peg and the dogs already settled in, though my aunt was actually sleeping in a Bed and Breakfast place across the road. The cottage had only two bedrooms. I would sleep on a camp bed on the sitting-room floor. 'What's Dad gone and done?' my father kept mocking himself as he squeezed from room to room, but in fact he was in the highest possible self-congratulatory spirits about the move he had accomplished.

My mother was also in a good mood and was pleased to have her sister there to share the novelty.

Outside, the cottage was like hundreds of others on the island, constructed of big stones crudely coated with whitewash. Inside, it was a strange microcosm of an upper-class English home. I was surprised at the amount of furniture that had been crammed into such a small space. The filing cabinet was there. So was a brand-new television. With untypical extravagance, my father had insisted on a 26-inch model and this was given a prominence the set had never been allowed in Wiltshire.

My father – still rigged out in squire's gear of flashy check jacket, waistcoat and corduroys – sat musing by the fire.

'I don't think the dogs are well. They have had a great shock. Tigger's got terribly thin.'

His attention then turned to one of the larger pieces of furniture. 'At Parkfield, that chest was just a tiny object in a huge house.'

These musings were followed by speculations about his fellow citizens on the island. Most of his dealings at this stage were with professional people – Mr Quayle of the Bank, the local garage owner, the vicar, a farmer named Teare from whom they bought eggs and milk, the doctor with whom they had already registered and a select handful of tradesmen.

'I'm trying to avoid running up a multitude of small accounts with shops,' my father explained.

His circle of social contacts was still very small indeed. A retired couple named Smith, whom he had known long ago in the North of England, were only of marginal interest, owing to what he saw as Mrs Smith's drinking problems. Then there was his old Wiltshire neighbour, Mr Parker, who had been so helpful during the move. Parker was spending Christmas on the island and my father had already played with him at the local golf club – 'This is top golfing country, you know' – and lunched with him twice at a hotel in Douglas.

Socially, that was about it so far, but my father was rapidly learning the names of local farmers, local millionaires and other significant figures.

That Christmas, my father was full of confidence and cockiness and there were even signs of increased harmony between my parents. Cottage life suited my mother. My father did not have to shout in these small rooms and there were no back quarters for him to thump or crash about in.

The presence of Aunt Peg did not upset him. My aunt sat awkwardly by the fire and, though taking everything in, remained quiet and thus provided an extra audience for my father's fooleries.

On Christmas morning, my father showed off by flamboyantly sharpening the carving knife, one of his few practical skills.

'You didn't know I could sharpen knives and razors, did you, Peg? D'you know I could always earn a living going round the barber shops in the West End of London sharpening razors? There are very few people who can do it.'

At a quarter past ten we climbed into the Rover and set off for a church high on the cliffs some distance away.

'This road was made for the Royal Air Force,' said my father proudly. 'This is all government road.'

Never a great one for noticing country things, my father surprised me by saying, 'Those sheep are huddled, William.'

When arriving anywhere by car, my father liked to order his passengers out and then park the car by himself. This time he was too hasty and my mother and Aunt Peg shrieked in unison, 'We can't get out. The car's still moving!'

As we walked solemnly towards the church, my father's feet crunching in the gravel, he told Aunt Peg, 'I've already bought grave space here for us both.'

The service in the small plain church with simple varnished pews was conducted by a clergyman with a Cockney accent. My father was already prepared to cross swords with him, on the familiar grounds of the church's coldness.

'How can that man expect people to worship in conditions like that?' he said afterwards, adding, 'I shall raise this thing with the bishop,' – and striking a Quakerish note – 'Christianity includes being business-like in all matters,' when my aunt and mother protested.

After lunch, my father said, 'Will you pass the port, which is immediately behind you?' and reached out for two cigars. However, he soon swept the decanter away – 'This is very good port and we're not going to be immoderate about it' – and fussed over what I was doing with my cigar ash.

'You're not putting your ash in the coal bucket, are you? Because coal is explosive. I'm very anxious not to have a fire here.'

As usual I gave my father a book for Christmas and he took it out of its wrapping in an automatic way, knowing that I was bound to have given him some reading matter.

'My God, it's cold,' he said later, putting aside the new book and announcing to the household, 'I shall now put on my long pants. With a good deal of ceremony.'

My mother and Aunt Peg huddled together over the fire, remarking how lovely it was. Their nostalgic, sisterly talk concerned old pets – 'I remember Betsy Bedlington gulping down Spratt's Ovals without chewing them at all'; 'I remember Binkie once caught a rat by its tail. The tail came off with three inches of pink innards' – comic incidents of the past – 'How we laughed about that, how we roared about that!' and eventually settled upon my grandmother, spending Christmas alone in her old folks' home, increasingly frail but never actually ill.

'Granny never catches flu,' said my mother.

Here my father, long pants now protruding from the bottom of his trouser legs, chipped in, 'Granny is made of the toughest teak,' and when the two sisters started criticising their mother's current state, suddenly leapt to the defence of his former house guest: 'Oh, Granny still says some wise things, doesn't she?'

*

During the next few days, my father's mood became increasingly retrospective, and he reviewed his life with considerable satisfaction. He looked back on his time at the Board of Trade with complacency and insisted there was nothing strange about his early retirement. 'I gave in my notice a year in advance. There was never any suspicion of my being sacked.'

His interest in London as he had known it had never been keener. He talked often of metropolitan life, city business circles – 'You don't even know who Ikey Wolf is, do you?' – and of the time he had bought Max Miller a drink. He continued to thumb through the London Atlas, which remained his favourite book. The streets of North Kensington, its pubs and people, were his primary interest. 'I would like one of my sons to have a good working knowledge of London,' he said, 'because I've been so fond of London all my life.'

He also looked back on the various houses he had lived in, before and after his marriage, with a mixture of pride and distaste. 'Ash Tree House was just a senior clerical workers' house . . . Crinkley Court . . . we did jolly well to get in there . . . Parkfield . . . Parkfield was a Victorian town house of good style. Don't you long for the pitch-pine atmosphere at Parkfield and Aunt Dot living within the pound?'

He also reviewed the careers of his sons with satisfaction. 'Richard was in the best regiment of them all . . .' he began, and he waffled on about Tim's exceptional talents and Edward's likely climb to the top of his bank and beyond. To his colonial middle son he was in fact writing a sycophantic letter which stated, 'I am delighted you have managed your private money so well.'

For me, he was content to reserve his judgment. My mother took my precarious existence with terrible seriousness, but my father was now unconcerned, preferring to make jokes about it.

'Everything all right at the bank, William?' he asked. 'From what I hear you'll be very pleased indeed to receive parental help for the next few years.'

It was most unlikely that the bank manager had said anything about my overdraft, but my father loved to pretend he was in the know about all his sons.

As well as looking back in this rambling manner my father also looked ahead calmly. 'In nine years' time, Mother will be seventy . . . I have an expectation of fifteen years. Of course we may be faced with very heavy nursing expenses . . . You may have an invalid parent on your hands at fifty pounds a day . . .'

*

The immediate task on my father's plate was to find a larger house on the island. He had already inspected two or three and rejected them. He was looking for a four or five bedroom property, with a little land of its own. He was willing to consider derelict properties as well as newly renovated ones and, if the former, would prefer a house built of bricks rather than stone.

'Tinkering around with brick is always easier than it is with stone,' he said.

Two days after Christmas he took us all, including Aunt Peg – whose advice on anything connected with farms or farmland he pretended to value – to have a second look at a deserted property called Ballagarret, close to the sea.

'This is the bitterest of all winds,' said my father when

we got out of the car, 'because of course it comes from the north east.'

After we had wandered round the property a few times, my father said he had firmly decided against it, on the grounds of the absence of winter sun.

Suddenly, he had become fascinated by the sun.

'It's a strange thing,' he said, 'to have lived to this great age without finding out about the path of the sun in winter.'

If thwarted in his search for the right house, he warned us he would seriously consider buying a flat in Douglas. He had soon mentioned this miserable alternative so often that he abbreviated it to 'a flat in Doug'. Here at least, he argued, there would be some guaranteed sun.

'Modern flats are built on a cruciform shape,' he explained. 'There's usually some sun for everybody at some time of the day.'

He continued to flatter Aunt Peg by seeking her opinion about various aspects of country life and in exchange gave her unsolicited advice on dentists and health in general. When his sister-in-law was absent, however, he poked fun at her.

'Poor old Peg has had a bad night,' he said one morning when she appeared from her lodgings across the road.

Towards the end of the visit my father began to show signs of his old irritation.

'I'm not sure Peg isn't on the threshold of another nervous breakdown.'

'If only he would treat your mother better, I'd be quite happy,' was Peg's counter-attack.

He was also losing patience with me or with the television that I kept trying to watch.

'Do you mind turning that thing right down so that you alone can see and hear. This is not a dance hall.'

A few minutes later he said more aggressively, 'Turn that TV off. Or I'll disgorge the whole thing.'

*

By the time of my departure, harmony between us had been restored, and for Aunt Peg too, he had some kind words.

'Goodbye, Peg. Come again whenever you want to. Oh, do take my advice, Peg. I've made a life study of dentists. Do go to a good dentist.'

The dogs danced at our feet.

'They think they're going back with me,' said Aunt Peg. 'That's very flattering.'

She was already oriented towards her Cumbrian cottage. 'My Aga stays half on when I'm away so the kitchen'll be fairly warm,' she said as my mother drove us to the docks.

I spent the next four hours crossing the Irish seas with my aunt and did not part from her until we reached Liverpool. I took a taxi across the crowded city to Lime Street station. Peg said she could easily walk to Exchange Station. A few minutes later in the city centre, I was surprised to spot her standing on a traffic island, head held high.

2

I did not visit the island for several months. I kept in touch with my parents and occasionally chatted about them with Richard and Tim. In February Tim visited the island and came back with some fairly predictable news.

'Father's just as irritable as ever,' he said.

In one of our increasingly rare meetings, Richard pronounced that the whole family, with the exception of Tim, was now on the decline. Ben's lively existence and dramatic death had become increasingly unreal though it was less than a year since his engagement and its tragic sequel.

From the Isle of Man came letters. My mother wrote of 'really horrid weather' but added that the Wigtownshire coast and Cumbrian mountains were visible on good days.

My father also wrote of the howling wind – 'The power lines are not taut and are flicking about. It may be safer not to have too much rigidity' – and added that the two family telescopes were now being refurbished by nautical opticians in Liverpool.

He also wrote obliquely: 'Mother passed her medical test last week, you will be relieved to hear,' and of Richard's likely change of job. 'I think a move is likely within the next few months. The alternative is Belgium – perhaps for the rest of his life.'

At the end of March my father wrote triumphantly, 'Mr Sweet informs me that I am no longer deemed to be resident in the UK.'

In spite of bad weather my father was still pursuing an outdoor life. 'I am getting golf regularly with a man who was Public Trustee in Uganda,' he wrote. 'A good player and I like him. One of his grandsons is mixed-race.'

He did not expand on this last point, but his letter two weeks later, announcing that Edward and his family were expected in early June, included more comments on this emotive matter.

'I played golf yesterday with the night porter at one of the big hotels in Douglas and from what he said other accommodation for Edward, Michiko and T. is desirable. There is more tolerance in London, I do think, but not here.'

In his next letter, he wrote 'Edward and Co. will have a

double room at Mrs Christian's Private Hotel. Twenty-five shillings each and nothing for Toby.'

*

I had partly forgotten what Edward looked like. His face was now yellow-brown and his wavy black hair was smacked firmly down on his head, the high neat parting maintaining his old-fashioned scholarly look. Beside him at Heathrow was Michiko, perky, excited and unruffled by the long journey and beside her in a collapsable pushchair was their baby son. Edward embraced me aggressively. I recoiled – much as I had done from my father's clumsy bear-hugs – and fell into a more formal pecking embrace with my tiny sister-in-law and my first close examination of my new nephew, now eleven months old and dressed in what looked like American baby clothes.

Edward's presence in London – they spent three or four nights at Richard's new house before flying to the Isle of Man – had a disruptive effect. I was beginning to build up a life for myself – at last – and Edward's anachronistic presence was difficult to accommodate. Edward had left the family circle six years earlier but now tried to demand the full attention and affection of the brothers he had abandoned. His jokes belonged to another era, centring often on Gilda, the dog who had presided over our teenage years but who had died during my parents' last few weeks in Wiltshire. He was largely ignorant of the new Liberated London and when we went to a restaurant together he handled the waiters with an old-fashioned severity which distressed me.

In other respects, he had become much more streamlined. His physical awkwardness and the spikiness of his limbs – Ben used to say that you could burst a balloon on Edward's elbow – had been harnessed and insulated. His once clumsy feet were now expensively shod and when they met my shabby loafers under a table withdrew neatly. His tailoring was now immaculate and he also splashed on a lot of after-shave lotion and spent a fortune on high-collared tailor-made shirts. When it came to opening his briefcase and locating a vital document, his long, bony fingers were surprisingly deft.

Over the years, Edward had acquired the manners of a businessman and seemed unable to rid himself of that particular style of speech. Even his brothers were sometimes treated like colleagues – or adversaries.

'That's fair enough,' he would say. 'I'll cross that one when I come to it.'

If I attempted to tell a joke, he would laugh in an exaggerated way – as he might at a colleague's witticism – or occasionally wait until I had finished and then tell me he knew it already.

In contrast, Michiko's affectionate and respectful attitude towards the family into which she had married was almost unnerving. She did not articulate her feelings but made a sort of humming noise whenever my mother, father, grandmother or aunt were mentioned, and she was unwilling to hear any of them abused even in the smallest way. Indeed when Edward or any of her brothers-in-law said anything at all critical about our elders and betters, Michiko went into another sort of trance and a more hostile hum came from her mouth.

*

The reunion with Edward and Michiko was brief. After a few days, they all flew to the Isle of Man and I went by train to Cumberland where I stayed with Aunt Peg and visited my grandmother. I found the oldest member of my family sitting in the sun outside her nursing home. She was perfectly groomed and still spoke in the decisive, alert tones of a woman who had once chaired meetings.

'My dear, I heard you were coming and I was looking out for you,' she said in the voice I had known all my life.

Though she was now ninety-three, my grandmother still tried to pamper me.

'We can give you some tea, you know. Are you sure you're warm enough?'

After a few minutes on the bench, my grandmother said, 'I think it's getting rather cold. We must go in and get a good set of biscuits,' and we shuffled together into the building and into her private room, where the only personal possessions were the pictures of Aunt Peg and my mother as children. Here an orderly helped my grandmother off with her coat.

'D'you want it in the wardrobe?'

'Er, No, On the door.'

When we were left alone, my grandmother continued to indulge me. 'Under the washpan, there's a chair. I keep that for all the visitors. That's right. Have you any time you must keep to? Now then, biscuits. There's a tin in that cupboard. See what you can find. Take some sweets too. I think I'll wait for tea. What are you going to do now? I don't mean this minute. D'you know when Peg's coming?'

Finally she said, 'My dear, thank you for coming. It's been very, very nice. Where's your car?'

'I haven't got a car,' I replied. 'I came by train.'

'Oh, of course. You never have had. I remember now.'

*

'Granny may go to a hundred and ten,' said my father when he collected me at the docks later that month, but his attention soon returned to his colonial middle son, who had just been staying with him. 'Now of course Edward is better off in income than we are. And that is the way I like to see it,' he said as we drove northwards.

This second visit to the cottage was less easy than the first. My father's cantankerous side had re-surfaced and the cramped conditions of the house were a cause of friction. Our bodies often touched and my father was obsessed by the fact that Richard, while putting on a jersey during a recent visit, had broken the overhead light with his elbow.

Now my father knelt uncomfortably at his filing cabinet. 'Do you mind not speaking to me while I'm going through a file? You would, wouldn't you?'

Outside it was nicer. My mother had already made a success of the little garden. Flies and bumblebees settled on the thriving plants she had brought from Wiltshire and there was even a small patch of lawn where my father had rolled about with his latest grandchild, Toby. The atmosphere improved further when the three of us and the one surviving dog – 'Come on, it's not too difficult, Tommy! Try!' – walked down to the sea and strolled along a vast empty shore under a pale sun.

My father's renewed irritability related to his failure to find the house of his dreams and to his growing dissatisfaction with his new neighbours. The farmers were all right. When an overloaded cart of hay went past the cottage my father exclaimed 'By Jove, look at that! 'Strewth, it's old Teare driving!' but he was disturbed and disappointed by his fellow tax exiles and brooded constantly about those he had met.

'I mean Richard was a little bit horrified by the class of cattle here,' he said and selected for special disapprobation a man he had met with his old Wiltshire neighbour Parker.

'God Almighty!' he fumed. 'Is he representative? Ghastly Wallasey accent!'

Parker himself was no longer an honoured figure. In fact my father greeted with some apprehension the news that this old acquaintance was now thinking of living permanently on the island himself.

My father's old north country acquaintances, the Smiths, had also proved a disappointment. Algie Smith was all right but his wife was now, in my father's eyes, quite obviously an alcoholic. This friendly couple had invited us to lunch and Mrs Smith had shown no sign whatsoever of this weakness, but my father had stuck to his guns. Driving off afterwards, he said solemnly, 'She's now going to drink herself to death. If you doubled back there at four o'clock you would find her drunk. No, she is drinking. She'll be drinking now until she goes to bed. There's no doubt at all about that.'

My father's social antennae were in full operation. He sniffed out scandals, raged on about the Christian-naming at the golf club and acted suspicious of the background of everyone he met.

As always, my mother remained oblivious to these prejudices, but she was less passive than in the past and frequently defended the island and its residents against my father's criticisms.

'Sheerrt up!' my father growled as she tried to interrupt one of his monologues and then shouted, 'Where's my tea? Look, I'm dying for tea!'

At six o'clock I put the television on for the News.

'Why? Why? Why?' said my mother on hearing that work on the American nuclear bomb was proceeding. My father was more concerned with the style of the reporter's tailoring. 'Now that's what I call a very cheaply cut suit.'

When a film followed the News my father's attention remained superficial and he was upset when the camera moved away from an attractive blonde.

'She's quite a good-looking – I want to see her! No, that's quite a good-looking woman.'

My mother then began yawning in an extreme way, sounding quite desperate, but my father got more involved in the film, even to the point of excitedly remarking, 'A fantastic piece of bluff!' A further fresh dimension entered our conversation the following day when my father tried to cross-examine me about the new girl in Tim's life.

'Is she an Honourable?' he asked.

'No, no, no,' I replied.

'Not?' said my father in mock surprise.

3

I had been aware of Tim's relationship with Catherine Cameron for a year or two. At some stage, he had shown me a photograph of her and said, 'That's the girl I'm crazy about,' but I thought no more about it. Now he told me that they were going to get married.

Richard was 'absolutely thrilled' by the news, but my own pleasure was mingled with the realisation that I would have to leave the flat and find a new home. 'These must go,' said Tim, in a terrifyingly casual gesture at the pictures by Ben which covered my walls. 'Poor Will,' he added more sympathetically and went on to say that he and his bride would go immediately on a world trip, including visiting her cousins in New Zealand, and therefore I could return to the flat for a while after the wedding.

This took place at the end of October. My mother and father arrived from the Isle of Man on separate flights and stayed in separate places. My father was in top form throughout the celebrations, partly because he had discovered that his new daughter-in-law was the grand-daughter of a Field Marshal.

Edward and Michiko were absent. I acted as best man and thus played a central role in the ceremony in which Tim moved smoothly from bachelorhood to married life.

4

'You're back in the nest,' said my father when he telephoned me at the flat a few days after Tim and Catherine had set off on their extended honeymoon.

He had meanwhile found a new nest for himself. After many months of searching he had bought a farmhouse with twenty acres round it in the same part of the island as his cottage. He hoped to be in by the New Year.

Richard had already seen the house from a distance and pronounced it an agreeable surprise.

'I must say,' he said when I telephoned him to discuss this development, 'I didn't see it apart from standing on a bank – I wasn't allowed to see it – but it looks impressive. We walked up Mount Golly or something, Mummy and I, the most lovely walk on the hill, and took a telescope and looked straight down at the house. It looks a little dull from that distance, but, er, impressive, I thought.'

The acquisition of this miniature manor house from a bankrupt Manx farmer was a new feather in my father's cap and when I visited the cottage for the last time in November, I found him excitedly chatting up some local dignitary on the telephone, buttering him up and talking all the while about his new home.

'There may be some delays in getting into the property. It's a ticklish matter. I intend to live over here for the rest of my life. I have bought what is called Gollybelly Estate. I am not a farmer in the true sense of the word. They're taking action against him in court on Tuesday. We're not anxious to have him at the lodge gates . . . Mr Quayle has this matter in hand with the creditors . . . And of course I shall be supporting to the full the Isle of Man Forestry Board. I've already bought gates from them and they are being assembled . . . As a retired English solicitor . . . May I leave it in your hands, sir? I'm spending about five thousand on the house over the next two years. I'm up against various forms of dry rot and things like that . . . When will you come and see us, sir? Mr Teare, who lives opposite and is really the leading man in the hamlet here, will tell you about me . . .'

The wind was in my father's sails again. Building work was one of his favourite activities . . . and now he had a big task on his hands and the prospect of labourers to boss around while his new home was being refurbished.

He was already lining up his team of builders and would do all the designing himself.

'Architects earn too much,' he said. His five years on the hospital board had prejudiced him against this profession. 'We paid out two hundred thousand to one firm of London architects for Torbay Hospital. A very high figure for purely paper work. I'm not having an architect near that place.'

*

In the spring of 1971, I visited them in their new home. The house was lovely, softly set in its own fields, approached by a short overgrown drive and surrounded by a cluster of disused farm buildings and trees. Unchanged for more than a century, it had been used as a parsonage at some time and had a grand front door and fancy scroll work at roof level. Inside it had a large kitchen, two small reception rooms, five bedrooms, one bathroom and a pretty curving staircase. It was a potted manorhouse, secluded behind hedgerow after hedgerow.

My parents were as pleased with their new home as I was and kept noticing further, mostly agreeable things about it.

'We're only twenty-one miles from Scotland, this house.'

'The day's improving. I can see the hills.'

'Catherine's parents don't think we live in a great bungalow up a tarred drive, do they?'

'Oh, this is so pleasant.'

'These floors were laid down before waterproof concrete was invented.'

A fire burned in the grate of one of the reception rooms, which also accommodated my father's bed, complete with double mattresses and chamber pot, and the television set. 'I shall sleep here until my room is ready,' said my father.

Around the house lay furnishings, fabrics, carpets and paintings that had been in store for the last fifteen months. Familiar objects I had known since my childhood lay propped against the walls. The carpets I had known were being re-fitted, the dark blue one from my father's bedroom in Wiltshire would be re-cut to fit his bedroom here. In the bathroom I found a load of old medicine bottles, many of which bore the label of the chemist my father used in Wiltshire. Zinc and starch powder; Rexall's Bone and Nerve Liniment; The Mixture. One bottle dated back over twenty years and carried the name of the chemists in Lancaster where my father's family had lived for so many generations.

Many of the larger pieces of furniture were on their way to Richard's new house where there was plenty of room.

Luckily my father had hung on to the old oak pieces, the sideboard and old armchairs, which suited the new house perfectly.

So far, so good, but my father was planning to make substantial changes to this gentle and rustic abode. Bulky storage heaters would be installed in the downstairs rooms, a bedroom would be converted into the essential second bathroom, and a new three-tier filing cabinet would be installed in the room he had earmarked as his office. Double glazing would soon render the old shutters inoperable and the room in which we now sat would be fitted with a double ceiling. A heavy brass chandelier would hang from reinforced woodwork on the staircase.

The process had already begun. Already a builder was at work, removing the old front door.

'Convenient to come in, Mr Quiggin?' asked my father, seeking permission to enter his own house.

Already my father's personality had changed. The new house was big enough for him to be jumpy again. Now he was shouting and asking his old questions – 'All right, William?' – not only to me but also – 'All right, Mr Quiggin?' – to the builder.

For some reason he chose to misunderstand my criticisms of his modernisation programme.

'We're not going to have any fancy trimmings here and that's that,' he said.

From time to time he would tease my mother by praising another property he had seen and rejected.

'But you people don't realise, it would have been jolly sunny!'

After dinner he relaxed a bit and announced, 'The time has come to Light Up.'

My father smoked his cigar to the hilt and kept it plugged into his mouth whereas I waved mine about.

'Where are you putting your ash, Richard – I mean William?'

My mother also interfered by fingering the saucer I was using as an ashtray and asking, 'Have you finished smoking? Can I wash that?'

In the playfulness that the cigar induced, my father began talking about the house being haunted.

'That bedroom of yours does have a history but I didn't mean to tell you.'

'It does not have a history!' exclaimed my mother.

In the morning I found my father puzzling over the absence of Quiggin, the builder – 'This is rather queer. Unless of course the chap is ill' – and then settling down to a long, jerky telephone conversation with a neighbour about borrowing his gardener.

'I'm frightfully sorry to bother you. Good morning sir. I'm frightfully sorry to bother you. What does your chap charge? Well that's perfectly reasonable. If you've got a minimum charge I'm perfectly ready to pay it . . . I had two part-time men in Wiltshire . . . Once I get my own mower. The grass I should think is now seven inches long. He allowed the grass to grow on the inner drive. A most extraordinary state of affairs! Sodium Chlorate will kill it eventually but there is stuff that will kill it stone dead, isn't there? Yes, well I know. Jolly good. Yes, well I'll pick up everything I can from him. Do come in and be our first visitors . . .'

After three or four days in this new environment, I found it a wrench to leave.

Letters followed from both my parents.

'The house is growing on us and we are both very happy,' wrote my mother.

'Mother loves this place and so do I,' wrote my father.

The only off-note was struck by Richard.

'They may have taken on too much,' he announced.

5

A few weeks later I had an unexpected call from Aunt Peg to tell me that my grandmother had died.

There was no grief from my aunt on account of the final demise of the woman whom she blamed so vigorously for blocking her development. On the contrary she was extremely excited at the prospect of filling her cottage with relations for the funeral.

My grandmother's death had been well prepared for, her grave space had been selected more than fifty years earlier and Granny herself had been saying for as long as I could remember that she was longing to die. Her life over the last few years had been increasingly difficult and her last weeks had been spent in a kind of cot, causing Aunt Peg to reflect, 'How are the mighty fallen!'

The Times announced that the funeral would take place at 2.30 a.m. the following Monday, but I ignored this eerie misprint and telephoned my aunt to say that I would be arriving shortly before lunch that day.

'I'll come and meet you,' said Peg, who had been cheated out of the big house-party she longed for. Tim and Catherine were still abroad, my father was unwilling to leave his new home, and Richard had said that he would travel there and back by sleeper, thus not spending the night under his aunt's roof.

Peg's only house guests were my mother and myself. My mother was in a graver mood than her sister and the solemnity she had inherited from my grandmother was most apparent as she moved from the crowded church to the graveyard full of red sandstone tombstones – and finally watched the coffin descend into the space allotted for it so many years ago beside the remains of her husband.

Peg had made very little attempt to tidy up her cottage for the tea-party afterwards, but the big table in her kitchen had at least been cleared and this was laid out with heavy silver spoons and forks, pieces of melon and lettuce leaves. My mother had quickly reverted to calling my grandmother 'an old dear', but Peg remained fairly disloyal though she had her usual fund of stories.

'But the funniest thing that happened was when Granny and I bought each other identical Christmas presents at the same shop! Bath towels! Wasn't that extraordinary?'

Richard seemed irritated by the atmosphere. 'William, can you fix that door?' he snapped and as so often before tried to treat his hostess as if she was an ordinary mortal. 'Aunt Peg! Do you know the number of Carlisle Station?'

There was a tense moment when the elderly solicitor present handed my mother a copy of my grandmother's will and said, 'There's nothing in it you didn't know already.'

That night in Peg's bathroom I came across the letter that my father had sent my aunt the previous week. It had already collected a number of stains and bore the imprint of a cat's paw.

'I shall remember Granny for her kindness to us during the War and during her last active years in Wiltshire when I hope that on the whole she was happy after leaving Cumberland where she was so loved by all.'

The letter ended by explaining that he would not be attending the funeral. 'Men are here every day and I must remain but Richard and William represent me.'

6

Shortly after my grandmother's funeral, Tim and Catherine returned from their honeymoon and took up residence in Chelsea at last. I fled, first to a lodging house down the road, from which I could see Tim drawing his curtains at night, then to a basement flat five streets away. This I was to make into my permanent home and the depository for my few possessions. My new sister-in-law helped me with the move, carrying the eighty volumes of *Punch* in the back of her car, swinging round the corners so fast that several were torn out of their bindings.

I kept in touch with Tim and Catherine, calling at the studio to pick up letters or summoned by Tim because there was a package for me. I also saw Tim around Chelsea and was once on the top of a bus which followed his estate car up King's Road, the frames, blank canvases and general mess in the back of the vehicle making it instantly recognisable.

Our encounters remained tense. I often visited or telephoned at the wrong time and found my brother flustered or otherwise occupied. Sometimes he was blunt and impatient – 'I've got an immense amount to do' – and at other times he was waspish – 'If that's all you've rung up to say, you must be very bored.'

Like Richard and Sally, they both showed little interest in my life. Indeed Tim often teased me by referring to the advertising business upon which I had turned my back two or three years earlier but which he pretended I was still working in. Exceedingly modest himself and most reluctant to accept praise for his work, he was also difficult to impress. If I was foolish enough to boast about a wonderful time I was having, Tim would quickly put me down – 'You could have fooled me' – and when I told him I was off to interview a famous actress offered me his sympathy – 'Bad luck!' Catherine was less subtle, exclaiming 'That creep!' when I sang the praises of some celebrated character I had met.

In spite of these tensions, I saw Tim and Catherine quite often, and when they were away Tim entrusted me with looking after his studio and dealing with urgent correspondence. In their absence the studio and flat became stale and unattractive but I sometimes lingered there, pondered over letters from satisfied clients – 'It was a stroke, if I may say so, of absolute genius' – or paused in the bathroom where there remained a tile that Ben had adorned with a surrealist image of a human foot and head.

*

My meetings with Richard and Sally were much rarer and the telephone calls that preceded them more drawn out. Richard had now changed his job as my father had predicted and was in a sort of marketing firm where he was protected by secretaries. 'He says he'll ring you back,' I was sometimes informed. At other times I was given a full account of his movements. 'He's in and out. He's flying up to Newcastle at seven-fifteen in the morning but he's got to be back for a meeting at three o'clock in the afternoon.'

When I telephoned him at home, I was more likely to get a child or the nanny. 'He's gone golfing,' said the nanny one weekend. 'He should be back about tea-time.'

When I telephoned again the girl informed me, 'I know they are going out to dinner about eight.'

When Sally herself answered the phone, her first 'Hello' sounded more uninterested than ever but she dealt with my enquiry as to Richard's whereabouts with the polished, cool efficiency of a woman married for ten years.

'He's in the bath. I'll get him to call you before he goes out.'

'It doesn't matter. I'll ring him tomorrow.'

'Are you sure? Because he can give you a quick buzz if it's not going to take hours and hours.'

I finally got through to my brother at three o'clock on a Sunday afternoon. Jubilant cries of children echoed in the background. 'I'm being entertained to a show,' he explained before plunging into his usual despondency. 'I'm rather tired. I ate too much for lunch.'

His gloom was far greater when eventually, after a break of six months, we met for lunch. His grunts, groans and yawns were matched by his thick brown corduroys and dark green jersey.

'Tim seems in good form,' I said.

'Yes,' he replied flatly.

Richard's relationship with Sally remained unknown terri tory but superficially they were completely loyal to each other and after lunch my brother said, 'Did you thank Sally for the meal?' and then carried a large silver cigarette box and heavy ashtray into the garden where there was a wooden bench.

'I feel so tired I really am quite worried about myself,' he began.

It was a relief when the telephone rang and he was summoned back into the house to answer a call from his friend Black who wanted to book him for a game of squash.

7

As Richard had pointed out, the family had now drifted into a lull. I continued to work asa journalist and my life began to expand in other directions, but in spite of these preoccupations I still visited my parents regularly, playing the role of the faithful son and accepting each new dose of provinciality offered by the Isle of Man without much reluctance or excitement.

My visits were preceded by telephone calls from my father, often late at night, as if he was trying to find out how and where I was spending my evenings. These began with a hiss of static and no reply to my initial 'Hello?' and then eventually, just as I was going to put the instrument down, my father would utter a long, slow 'Hallooo'. If I called him, he was even more cautious, picking up the telephone without saying anything and not speaking until he had established who was on the line.

After these playful preliminaries, he would plunge into the practicalities of my visit. 'Bring thick shoes and a raincoat' or 'Bring a dark suit' he would say, orders which would be echoed by my mother with a milder, 'Don't have your hair too shaggy.'

To reach my parents' new home required seven changes of vehicle and could take the best part of a day, and even a night if I missed a connection. These lengthy ordeals caused a build-up of resentment within me at the strange move my parents had made.

It was particularly frustrating that after such a journey my parents were usually not present when I finally stepped off the ship or emerged from the airport. The drive from the north of the island took less than an hour, but my father was not prepared to inconvenience himself to the extent of waiting for me. Even when he did appear, he never seemed very pleased to see me and as we left the airport or dock showed more interest in the other travellers and even exchanged words with them, while I trailed beside him unnoticed.

This ordeal was further prolonged by my father's habit of

leaving the Rover in some distant municipal car park, instead of ignoring the 'No Waiting' signs and quickly picking me up like everyone else.

'Gilda is in the car,' said my father one day as we set off together.

Gilda had been dead for two years, but my father continued to apply her name and gender to the surviving dog whose less distinctive name now sometimes evaded him, and when this animal eventually greeted me with squeals and squeaks my father looked on blankly.

I then climbed in and found on my seat a small heavy parcel marked 'E. Quine and Sons. Brassfounders and Locksmiths.'

My father's initial harshness usually lasted only a few minutes and by the time we reached the house he was in a more mellow mood. I now accepted that part of the point of my being there was for him to have someone to trample on.

'Where did that coat come from, may I ask?' he began. 'I know. The loco sheds at Lille.'

*

I would soon settle into the routine of the house and enjoy the pleasanter side of being under my parents' roof again, even in this strange outpost of the British Isles.

In spite of my father's modernisations, the house had retained its cosy charm. The sea wind shook the surrounding trees and whistled through minute cracks in the windows. Newly acquired clocks ticked and the fire full of foaming logs hissed like a small waterfall. The chairs were more comfortable than the sticks of furniture in my basement and I sank into them gratefully.

I was now more tolerant of the innovations my father insisted on making. Mr Quiggin was in the process of laying down 'a really fine oak strip floor' in the drawing room. There was the usual fussing over curtains and pelmets, and my father had acquired a new weakness for buying inferior antique clocks. Though these refinements were matched by the increasingly gruesome state of, for example, the telephone mouthpieces and lavatory bowls, I was now content to drift along with the regime, accepting sherry from a dirty glass if I were offered it and more willing than some of my siblings to put up with the chill of the house.

'The storage heater got knocked on by mistake when Tim and Catherine were here,' said my mother innocently.

The day started slowly with my mother giving me breakfast. Sausages, kippers, home-made marmalade and toast were served in the kitchen before my father came down, and there was an atmosphere of real leisure. My father's emergence ruffled the calm sea. Throughout the day he was never stationary for long. While my mother worked methodically in the kitchen, making only bumps and knocks, a knife being put down on formica, a spoon digging into a jar, my father crashed about, slamming doors, wrenching open drawers.

His restlessness was infectious. I moved about the house, smoked the odd cigarette, opened the occasional desk. One day I found a letter from my father's old flame, Bobbie, beginning 'I am still alive!! Are you surprised?!' but usually there was nothing to excite me. My father seemed aware of my movements and sometimes addressed remarks at me from another room.

'Smoking again?' His voice came from upstairs and then completely out of the blue, 'Mr Sweet tells me you're not saving.'

To my mother he would rap out occasional orders: 'Right! Coffee when you're ready.'

Eventually he would drive off to collect *The Times*, making his departure coincide with my mother serving lunch.

As the old Rover came crunching back later, the dog would bark madly and there would be a further delay before my father reappeared. Sometimes he had a solemn announcement.

'There's No *Times* On The Island.'

Afternoons followed a similar pattern. If he had obtained a newspaper he would settle down with it for a while, reading things aloud – 'Camellias one year old. Five for a pound' – or learning of the death of an old acquaintance. 'Admiral Towpath has died,' he announced one afternoon.

Deprived of a newspaper, he would tease the dog, drawing a fierce rebuke from my mother. 'If dogs are sleeping let them lie,' she would say for the umpteenth time.

Sometimes we would go to the sea. My father had now turned against the golf club on account of 'the ghastly Christian-naming' that went on there and preferred to practise his strokes alone on the sandhills near the sea. He was happy to do this in the fog and at all times of the year. He took a boyish interest in bad weather which reminded him of holidays with his mother in Cornwall long ago.

'Now that looks to me like a rough sea. I saw some fantastic seas in Falmouth as a boy.'

My mother was more interested in the lights winking from the Mull of Galloway – and in picking up driftwood to burn on the fire.

In the summer, we returned to the same stretch of beach, my father, in well-cut cream-coloured jacket and trousers, separating from us, his aluminium golf club glinting in the sun from a long way off.

Together again, I noticed my father gazing thoughtfully beyond me at a woman on the edge of the sea.

161

'Now that's a person who's bathing very sensibly,' he said. 'Very sensibly indeed.'

Back at the house, preparations for the evening meal often began with the drawing of a cork. My father took the business of airing wine seriously and carried the bottle to the fireplace with solemnity.

'William is demanding dinner tonight,' he explained.

'William, you may start your food now,' he would say later but the real focus lay on the end of the meal and the service of port and Stilton.

This was a cue for my father to disappear again, returning to fuss over the port glasses, juggle them around and sometimes find fault with them.

'I once went to a cocktail party in Chelsea and was given a glass with a chipped rim. I came away with a bleeding mouth.'

On at least one night of each visit there were also cigars. My father currently favoured a brand called La Tropicale de Luxe, obtainable in individual tubes, which he kept in a locked cupboard in the downstairs lavatory.

'I've never known a cigar smoke as well as this,' he would say.

Television accompanied and sometimes interfered with these rituals. It played a role in my parents' life it had never been allowed to before, and for my father it was an inspiration for lordly comments and cynical observations on his fellow men.

My father and I occupied the two big armchairs in front of the set while my mother, who had at first declined my seat, chose a much smaller chair – 'Little tiddler will do for me' – and sat there with the dog Tommy in a miserable pose on her lap.

'Where are my speckies?' she often asked at a key moment.

My father had already clipped his gold judge's spectacles on to his face and eyed the screen intently.

'Now that's the sort of chap who comes over here and I can't stand his guts.'

Variety programmes began well – 'Lovely bit of sax playing, that' – but my father accepted very few of the items that followed at their face value. Watching a pop star belting out her songs, he remarked 'She's doing all this for her children', and when one of this singer's children was featured running across a lawn, he added, 'Be at Harrow, later, that boy.'

When a comedian came on, my father commented, 'This chap has been involved in some very serious criminal matters. I don't suppose you knew that.'

A lifetime of careful newspaper reading had given my father all sorts of unsavoury information about the criminal, sexual, political and medical history of those in the public eye. I now played along with him and often asked him about the background of different people.

'Is Dingle Foot a socialist?'

'Oh yes. Terrible.'

My father's hatred of 'left-wing types' was now masked by a veil of self-mockery. One night he suddenly perked up when a documentary film about Germany came on.

'I had a very, very pleasant ten days in Berlin in 1934,' he began dramatically. 'I met a member of the National Socialist Party who was very keen on my being presented to Hitler.' He allowed this claim to sink in and then carried on speedily 'That-wasn't-possible-but, er, I did take out one night the daughter of the legal adviser to the Party.'

Later when the Führer himself came on the screen, my father first caught my attention and then made a solemn Nazi salute from his armchair.

Only during the News did he pipe down, but even then he was willing to drift off into a longish discourse inspired by the news-reader's suit.

'That's quite a well cut coat, you know, William. That's not the cheapest form of tailoring. That's not that dreadful form of what I call strip tailoring. Now I'd like you to have a suit like that. Jack Pratt's got a few dozen, I suppose.'

My father remembered my friendship with Jack and sometimes teased me about his unexpected success in the City of London.

The day would end with my father returning his gold spectacles to their case and disappearing into the backquarters of the house in search of a bottle of beer, a process marked by the banging of doors, the jerking open of drawers and the statement 'Good dog' to the sleeping pet.

Twenty minutes later, he might enter my darkened bedroom, puffing at a cigarette, to say a final goodnight.

As a rule, it was my mother who drove me to the airport or dock. We would leave the house together before my father was up and my mother would praise the Morris Minor – 'It's faster than it was. Since it had its insides out' – and curse the Rover – 'That old bus is a dreadful thing to manoeuvre.' Sometimes we would get stuck behind a stationary vehicle – 'I don't think this old toad is moving', or be dazzled by the early morning sun – 'All I can see is a ball of fire.'

8

My father had learnt with interest of my acquisition of a basement flat in Chelsea, and I had invited him to stay there when he next came to London. In due course he arrived for his first visit, clumping down the area steps with golf clubs and canvas holdalls, each item labelled with my address. For a few moments he barked at me excitedly but he soon became more thoughtful.

My new home, he said, reminded him of the tart's flat where he had lost his virginity. 'A basement just like this . . . it was all over in ten minutes of course . . .'

Within minutes of his arrival, he took off every stitch of clothing and, showing off his white, slightly hunch-backed body, advanced along the stone-flagged passage to the bathroom. He slammed the door shut in my face and shot home the bolt.

From the bath tub he soon shouted at the top of his voice, 'Yep?', though I had not said anything. His cry was a jubilant declaration of his joy to be back in London.

*

My father's presence in my flat had an invigorating effect. He was in and out all the time, driving himself quite hard, going off to play golf with Richard, attending appointments with the dentist who looked after his teeth for the past thirty years – 'He's given me what I call senior civil servant treatment' – and seeing his tailor, his shirtmaker, his solicitor and his accountant. He filled me in on his movements and discussed his various options with me.

'Burberry today or not?' he pondered one morning.

Then he counted the money in his wallet. 'The cupboard is bare except for . . . twenty pounds.'

Another day he showed me samples of cloth from which he was to choose the material for a new suit. One of them was an unlikely bright blue silk. 'You couldn't wear that, except at a swell luncheon party.' Finally he would set off, purposefully climbing the area steps and remarking without a backward glance, 'Lunch with Mr Sweet.'

Around tea-time he would return, equally bouncy and invigorated by his experiences. One afternoon a sprig of gypsy's heather protruded from his buttonhole. Another time, he carried a copy of the *Kensington Post*, a newspaper I had never considered buying, the purchase of which showed his continuing curiosity about the details of London life.

Then, without asking, he would help himself to the telephone. He would talk to his daughters-in-law and other sons, introducing himself as 'Grandfather'. His daughter-in-law Sally had avoided visiting the Isle of Man so far, using her children as an excuse, but my father had not given up trying to persuade her.

'You cannot come over to the island yourself? Well, obviously, with all these people you can't. But Richard, does he want to come over? No? Well, there it is.'

These family calls were followed by more bombastic conversations – 'Ah yes. Got it. Righto!' – with various tradesmen. Of the tailor, who had also made a number of suits for Richard, Tim and Edward, he said, 'He looks upon me as a patriarch who has brought him a lot of business.'

If I attempted to interrupt these calls my father would say tersely, 'My son is here making a lot of noise.'

Sooner or later, he would ask for refreshment and other essentials: 'You've got no ink here, have you?' I would make him tea and minister to him in various ways while our conversation flew in different directions.

'The deeper you dug the harder she got,' he said of his late mother-in-law, and when I argued that most people had a soft centre, he shocked me by saying. 'Your mother hasn't got one.'

*

Occasionally, we went out together to the pub on the corner, I had often visited this place on my own but the barman never seemed to recognise or greet me. My father, after only two visits, had already established a rapport with this man, who now greeted him enthusiatically the moment he strode through the doors.

'Hello, sir. How are you, sir?'

My father had often said that pubs were 'full of bounders and failures' but he liked them none the less and as we sat together on a padded corner seat, he reminisced about his pub experiences.

'I used to take Bobbie to places like this and she thoroughly enjoyed sinking a pint or two.'

Walking back to the flat, my father would stop and stare at the London scene as proud as a peacock and pronounce upon what he saw. Gazing at an apartment block with many lit up windows – we were now in the recession of 1974 – he said, 'They're all at home. They can't afford to go out.'

During daytime excursions my father often got involved with people on the street. Seeing a pretty woman with a small child getting out of a car, he leapt forward in a courtly manner and said, 'Oh may I, can I . . . ?'

He displayed the same courtesy when I took him upstairs to meet my landlady. A frail elegant woman in her sixties, she gave him tea and he admired her L-shaped drawing room.

'Tell her your father was a friend of Sir Flinders Guthrie,' he said later, and after further reflection, 'You might do a lot worse than . . . marry . . . upstairs.'

*

The jolly give-and-take that my father and I had at last established was now played out in the small basement flat.

'Delicious tea, as always here. Vair pleasant,' he said, but within moments was ordering me to turn off my radio.

'You're not an opera fan?' I asked, treating him for once as if he were a normal human being.

'No. Nor ballet,' he replied, his lip curling.

I played the role of my mother, even to the extent of using an old sock to keep his boiled egg warm.

'I'll tell you one thing,' he said as he discarded this article without comment and began to attack the egg. 'I've got the feeling Peter Sweet's going to get married again. I could be wrong.'

The topics he had kicked around all my life were still part of his repertoire, including his will, though his will-dangling was now more playful.

'In my new will,' he began one morning, 'you are to receive . . . my entire wardrobe . . . Now don't be a muggins and go and sell it all. It's probably the best wardrobe on the island. Apart from theatrical people's, of course.'

This strange harmony between us was cemented when, during his visit in the summer of 1974, he took me to dinner at the Ritz Hotel. He was still proud of his Manx financial status and this gesture was one of his few acts of un-Quakerly extravagance.

It was a warm evening – gnats entered the largely empty restaurant and got into my wine and hair. At the end my father paid the bill and wrote his address on the back of the cheque. 'That's an estate in the north part of the island,' he explained but the waiter looked blanker than ever.

After dinner we took a bus to Richard's house. We were surprised to find that Richard was not home, held up by an office party. Sally asked us if we would like a drink.

'We would,' said my father with unusual keenness.

A few minutes later, we heard the rattle of a taxi and someone fiddling with the latch of the front gate. Sally then opened the front door and sang out in clear accusatory tones Richard's full name, including his rarely used middle one.

Richard walked into the house like a doll, passed me and my father without saying anything to either of us and went straight upstairs. It was the first time I had seen my brother drunk – and Sally too, after her opening harangue, appeared anxious and solicitous to his needs, following him upstairs while my father and I retreated.

'She was protecting her marriage,' said my father when we reached my basement. 'After we'd left, I bet she went for him like a rattle-snake.'

The following morning, and for months afterwards, my father made the utmost of Richard's moment of weakness. First he had rung Richard's office and now he was on the telephone to Sally, who immediately assured him that Richard would not do it again.

'He's a very, very silly fellow if he does because he won't stay very long with these people. They won't want him. I've rung his works and he's not available until three o'clock. That's it, you see. Poor chap! Did the taxi need cleaning up? No? Better if he had been. Better if he had been sick. Well of course. I mean, look, he should have had a proper meal first. Or joined us at the Ritz. We had a damned good dinner and would have liked to have had him there. Providing he was in a gentlemanly state, of course.'

For the rest of the week my father constantly alluded to the incident, and when eventually he left he had a final thought on the matter.

'That thing the other night rather spoiled this visit.'

My father's departure left a gap in my life, and that night

I slept in the bed he had vacated, not bothering to change the sheets. Among the bedclothes I was pleased to find his hot-water bottle.

9

My weekend visits to the Isle of Man continued for the next year or two and were unruffled by major family crisis or setback. I had wondered if my father's character would mellow in his island hideaway but the reverse was the case. His eccentricity was snowballing. The mixture of oddness and extreme conventionality was undiluted.

During my visits, he seemed continuously over-excited. Lying on my bed and trying to read a book, I would hear my father's unbeautiful voice raised in one or other of the downstairs rooms, and in my presence he never gave up for a moment. Perhaps he had little to say, hence the continuous barking voice and the repetition of nonsense. Or was it the cry of a trapped animal who might bite if you tried to assist it?

Already lonely when he lived in Wiltshire, the decision to live on the island had enhanced his isolation. My mother remained shy and self-sufficient. My father craved human company – yet often shrank from it when it was offered. From time to time, he would repeat his familiar monologue about the dangers of close friendship, ill qualified though he was to make such remarks. 'Most people have three to six close friends,' he told me gravely, but I doubted if he had even one friend. He was certainly not friends with my mother. As Aunt Peg often pointed out, it was a master-servant relationship and my mother's passivity had long ago prevented the possibility of it ever changing.

He was not short of acquaintances and in his own limited way considered himself popular. 'It's not a bad island,' he remarked after he had been there a few years. 'We've got about nine friends and forty acquaintances.' He had certainly integrated himself into the strange community of uprooted middle-class people, ex-colonials, retired Indian Army regulars and tax exiles who shared the island with him, and was remarkably well-informed about their state of health.

'There's a lot of illness among the rich here,' he said, and he would go on to describe how one neighbour had gangrene of the hand, poor chap, another had had 'an unsuccessful operation on his private parts' and yet another was shortly to submit to a bowel operation, an undertaking which my father described as 'a bloody skulduggerous thing'.

He was superficially sycophantic to these people. One day I heard him sucking up to someone on the telephone. 'Please-accept-our-deepest-sympathy,' he intoned. 'I shall be represented at the funeral of course. You will be disposing of the house?'

He then announced solemnly, 'General Trotter has died.'

One summer my father took me to see the local flower show being opened by the wife of the Isle of Man's Governor. When this lady entered the tent, my father suddenly bowed very low, the only person to do so, and when during the same event my father met this personage he gushed at her. 'Oh, we did enjoy your party the other night. We enjoyed it beyond measure.'

The names of his neighbours' homes fell from his lips with a mixture of mockery and respect. 'Glen Doon', 'Ballamanor', 'Kerragaroo', 'Sholty-Gill' – some of these places may have been bungalows but my father spoke the names with reverence and even nodded vaguely in their direction as he did so. When I asked him where some new acquaintances lived, he replied with relish, 'Oh, Battywing is about two miles from here.'

In fact, my father looked down upon the majority of his neighbours.

'There are about fifty millionaires here,' he told me. 'And you will find most of them incredibly boring.'

Most boring of all, in his opinion, was a chap called Knife, 'a terrible looking little man' who employed four full-time gardeners but according to my father had 'a pronounced Lancashire accent, that sort of clipped north country accent'. When I pressed my father for details of Mr Knife's educational background, he replied dismissively, 'He was born in Morecambe and no doubt went to Morecambe Grammar School. That chap wouldn't have the slightest chance of getting into the Reform Club.'

His closest neighbours were a couple called Whittle. Mrs Whittle was the daughter of an electronics tycoon, but Captain Whittle, according to my father, had no money at all. 'Very few Service people have. Why should he?' he said impatiently. 'Whittle's shirts are terrible. He gets them from a multiple shirt maker in Bradford.'

Other neighbours included a man who owned a business in North Wales, a retired surgeon from Birmingham – 'Bloody rascal that man. He's a socialist' – and Mr Meekin, owner of a big garage in Ramsey. 'Meekin thinks I should live in a Staybrite Steel bungalow and buy a new car every year.'

In spite of his suspicious nature, my father continued to find new social contacts to toss and gore in his mind, though when I tried to play along with him, asking if such-and-such a person was a 'gentleman', he snapped back angrily, 'How could he be? A Truro builder's son!'

There was one neighbour against whom he had now turned completely. This was his friend from Wiltshire, poor old Parker, now a permanent resident on the island. Not only did my father refuse to see him but he spent much of his time fuming about him.

One reason was social. 'We've met some terrible people with Parker. He is a man who quite obviously has extremely second-rate friends,' explained my father. 'Much to my fury, the Governor said to me "I hear Parker is one of your oldest friends". I've had to write him a letter. "My dear Parker," I said. "Please don't misunderstand but really—".'

Another reason was my father's growing suspicion that Parker was 'a half-and-half chappie'. He kicked himself for not noticing it earlier – 'I now remember he came and sat on a sofa unnecessarily close to me after lunch.' His chatter about this former friend began with mere innuendos, but built up to a climax in which the word 'queen' was forcefully repeated.

*

My father's sense of superiority to Parker and the others I have mentioned was counter-balanced by a growing feeling of inferiority to another, newly discovered stratum of Manx residents. He had only recently become aware of the existence of a few isolated relations of the English and Scottish nobility and also of a handful of landowning Manxmen.

'There are only about twelve upper-class Manx families and they treat us with great reserve,' he said of this latter group.

During his first few years on the island my father had considered himself a big fish in a small pond, but this vision was now melting away as he became more and more aware of the presence of other, more formidable figures residing on the island.

Now he would list and re-list his upper-class neighbours in a long jerky monologue, a string of unfinished sentences, which he would repeat and revise during each visit I paid him.

'It's small but there is an upper class here,' he would begin. 'I'll tell you who the members of it are, shall I? Shall we start right at the top, north of here? The Giggles.' He let this meaningless name sink in and did not qualify it.

'Then there's Olivia Oceanbed. You can't get around that one, chum. She may not have friends here but in London – Well, then, you move down here to what I call the Northern Plain and you can't honestly say that Jack Knife, with his ghastly Morecambe accent – but when you get into Ramsey there's Lord Fuddle's daughter, Ian Poppy and the Marquess of – no, there are three marquesses on the island – Marquess of Middlingham – and of course the Chaplins. Now I can't tell you anything about the background of Jimmy Chaplin but his wife, well, that family has been brewing beer in Newcastle for two hundred years. The Honourable Anne Chaplin. She is obviously – her great-grandfather I daresay was no more important than my great-grandfather but – now then there's Pussy and Billy Wilson and the Miss Bobbins, Veronica and her sister, who live at Glen Doon. Their father was a baronet. A Derbyshire baronet. Then we come to Captain Pipkin of Ballamunster. The Pipkins are the Pipkins. I can't possibly tell you what sort of chap the grandfather was. Sir Geoffrey and Lady Teed? No! She was a nurse in Birmingham. Not particularly important socially. Lord Bird, Viscount Bird, who married a Manx lady, lives in Douglas. Lord Smellie of ICI, a man with no sense of humour whatsoever. Lord Pike. Is he a Catholic by any chance? I wouldn't be surprised . . .'

Eventually, as he approached the bottom of the island, the monologue would tail off and my father began to talk only of the island's richest tax exiles.

'The new man in The Quink is reputed to be worth five and a half million. Les Winterbotham is reputed to be worth two million but he only gave me a nasty cork-tipped cigarette after luncheon. Lady Potty is a woman worth ten or twenty million.'

'Does she mix?' I asked, getting a word in at last.

'No, she's just made fun of.'

*

From time to time, one or other of these people would ask my father for a drink or a meal, an invitation which he would accept with glee. He was happy to drive right down the island if the invitation came from the elite. The old Rover came into play again for these trips and there was high tension before departure, shouts of 'Coffee when you're ready, please,' and 'I'll be ready in about five minutes now.'

Sometimes the invitation was extended to include any son who might be staying, and several times I travelled with them down the island. My father drove slowly, especially to start with, doffing his cap at every passer-by. On the main road, he continued to point out upper-class homes and announced his likely bladder-emptying schedule.

'I shall be passing water around the Bishop's Palace.'

'As early as that?' said my mother.

'Well I don't know,' said my father, suddenly bored by the topic. 'As soon as the coffee comes through.'

At one such lunch party my father was dismayed to find among the other guests his wealthy neighbour, Jack Knife. His *bête noire*'s presence in a red tweed suit shook him up, and driving home afterwards he was disturbed to catch a glimpse of the millionaire's Jaguar coming up fast in the rear mirror.

'Knife wants to overtake,' he said nervously.

The presence of Jack Knife on this occasion, and his obvious intimacy with his hosts, forced my father to revise his opinion of the self-made businessman's status on the Northern Plain and before long he was remarking, with only a slight ruefulness, 'Knife is the top chap up here.'

*

At regular intervals, my parents themselves entertained. Their lunch parties were preceded by a lot of fussing about by my father, the popping of corks and the banging of doors.

'Now, *Manx Life*,' he said entering the room with a magazine of this name in his hand. 'We'll have that on the table. Just to show we're interested. Put that London paper away, William. Now these chairs, I don't know where they've got to. We'll all be standing up. Except Captain Pipkin of course. Tin tray, please. No, I'm not providing lemonade. Not at nine pence a lemon.'

These practical concerns were followed by serious warnings about my conduct.

'Miss Bobbin and her sister are not people to play the fool with. If you suddenly burst into sniggers it is likely to be taken very seriously indeed. Much more seriously than it would be in Wiltshire.'

Eventually there was a crunching sound as a car circled in the thick gravel outside the front door.

'I hear a car, Father.'

'I realise that, William.'

My father shot out of the house at high speed, his rakishly long tweed jacket flapping open as he welcomed the first of his guests almost before the car had stopped moving.

When the party was over, there was a post-mortem and close questioning of my conduct.

'You called him Sir, didn't you? Once? Captain Pipkin?'

On learning that one of his guests was a Roman Catholic, my father began making a low growling noise.

*

Social life brought out the best in my father. He was good at small talk, his eccentricities were harnessed. Back at his own fireside his old obsessions resurfaced. His anti-popery was relatively mild when compared with his interest in bodily functions and anything abnormal in the sexual area. References to wayward girls being chastised by nuns had often fallen from his lips, and I was now interested to find the biography of a famous lesbian beside his bed.

These unwholesome interests connected somehow with his lifelong concern with medical matters and dentistry. Dentistry was of special importance to him. A dentist was not only a person who looked after your teeth but a hierarchical yardstick by which he could measure his own and other people's social status.

'Dentists don't get into the better clubs in London. Public prosecutors do.'

Over and above these increasing interests in his own and other people's health was his obsession with money. His income had doubled or trebled since he had settled on the Isle of Man but there were no signs of extra cash or any release from the pressures he had begun to feel so keenly in Wiltshire. Our dinner together at the Ritz had been a rare event. Within seconds of getting up each morning until last thing at night his mind revolved round money matters, income and capital, his own and other people's.

'D'you know what this family's gross income is? You'd be jolly surprised if I told you.'

'Why have you got such a complex about money?'

'You're just talking very foolishly indeed.'

This sort of exchange took place often, but my relationship with my father remained harmonious. Only sometimes at breakfast might I be caught off guard by a sudden onslaught or by his relentless repetition of some ridiculous accusation.

In fact he showed little interest in my life and only in my journalism when I mentioned I might write an article on the Isle of Man.

'Something like that would do us untold harm.'

Instead, he made nostalgic remarks about my time in the advertising agency. 'If you'd stayed there, you could have built up pension rights by now,' he said. 'Oh, I wish I could get you back on a salaried basis.'

Occasionally he seemed to view my future prospects with gloom. 'In six months' time you'll be the age when I felt I was on top of things,' he said. 'You ought to be in the position to join a club by the time you're thirty.'

Preoccupation with his own ideas made him a bad listener and even my humblest attempts at conversation usually faltered, drawing a blunted 'Yep' or 'Nope' from him. More ambitious questions – 'D'you think there's life on other planets, Father?' – were met with complete silence.

From time to time, he would speculate about me in the third person.

'What William likes doing is spending his tax money in night clubs'; 'William mixes mainly with bedsitter and boarding house people'; 'I think William may be announcing his engagement sooner than some of us think,' and other remarks along these lines were designed to provoke a revelation or denial from me.

His rare questions about my social circle – 'Have you no

professional friends?'; Tell me, have you met any Quakers in London?'; 'Oh, by the way, any of your friends caught flu and had an awful time in single rooms?' – were equally wide of the mark.

Occasionally he would criticise my continuing bachelor status – 'They count for nothing, bachelors, after the age of thirty-five. And I'm not talking about living with women. That's no life at all. Never has been' – and tried to provoke a further response from me by suggesting that I was now going out with the Yorkshire lady who had been much in evidence at Ben's funeral.

'Oh, by the way, you're seeing quite a lot of that old tart, aren't you? Some sort of dreadful character, if she wasn't a prostitute.'

My father's comments on his other sons were equally barmy. He now spoke of the knighthood which awaited Tim – 'which I think could easily be the case' – and heaped praise on my sister-in-law Catherine.

'She worships him,' he gushed. 'She's one in a million.' His thoughts about Edward centred upon his healthy bank balance. 'Edward may be asked to repay his school fees to me,' he now postulated and went on, 'That little angel Toby will have money of his own soon.'

It was for his eldest son that he reserved most of his ridicule and he loved to dwell upon the weaknesses he had discovered in Richard's character. 'Why does Richard communicate so badly with his kith and kin? He's not drinking again, is he?'

These insinuations were temporarily eclipsed by some crazy speculations about Richard's chess and squash playing friend Black. During his last visit to London, my father had found this man having a bath in Richard's house and he was unable to forget the encounter and the fact that Black was still unmarried.

'What you don't realise,' he said, 'is that this chap Black has had a series of irregular relationships.'

Watching television later, my father suddenly piped up, 'Black was wearing a shirt like that when I saw him!' and continued to ponder upon the relationship between Black and his eldest son.

'I can understand a man being very fond of Richard,' he said, drumming his fingers on the table and trying to catch my eye.

*

My mother did not enjoy my father's peculiar postures but she had learnt to avoid them by sinking into a sort of slump, leading eventually to high-pitched yawning, or by leaving the room.

'I've got a tummy pain. I must take an indigestion tablet.'

She yearned for her bath and bed, though when she finally reached the end of the day she did not sleep any better than she had in Wiltshire and when I retired about two hours after her, I would hear the turning of the pages of a fishing magazine from her small single-bedded room.

In spite of this nightly forlornness, my mother continued to enjoy her new home. Within a few months she had created a small vegetable and herb garden with flint walls, which was now bursting with healthy produce. She was always happy in the garden, working on a bonfire or some simple task, while my father, whose interest in gardening remained limited to lawn maintenance and the planting of suburban hedges, stormed, crashed or shifted about uselessly.

'I've just seen a horrible big rat running beside the wall,' said my mother coming in from the garden. 'It wasn't going very fast. It was almost as if it were ill.'

My mother did not share my father's mocking attitude towards her children and although Tim remained her favourite son she was slow to praise his work and often critical of his use of the colour green. Long ago, my mother had been an accomplished artist herself – I had once found an unframed oil painting of a donkey's head – but she underestimated her talents and had given up this hobby on getting married.

Her attitude towards the neighbours was also far milder. Class distinctions did not worry her though she could not help being aware of my father's hatred of certain people and may have in fact shared some of his feelings. 'Father sees red when I mention Pam Gobstopper because she is so common and dull and dreadful,' she admitted, but of other of my father's *bêtes noires* she was tolerant – 'Whatever could be the harm in having Terry and Sue Whittle here?' she said almost in despair – but my father stuck stubbornly to his guns and projected his own prejudices onto his wife.

'Your mother doesn't want to get tied up with middle-class people like the Whittles and Colonel MacBogus. You'll get nothing out of being friends with common people.'

Her own description of their outings had a more generous ring. 'Mrs Giggle is a weather-beaten old thing but she is a lady. She's broken her neck twice out hunting. She has a very gaunt dining room. We started with rather a watery soup which I rather waded through . . . Mr Poppy has got a pink face with a little sandy moustache. He was cooking on a barbecue when we arrived. He has a super stereo system. His wife is charming and full of chat but not a beauty. She has curly hair . . . Lady Teed is just a sort of fat pudding saying all the right things. She said she'd been out to dinner on Friday and Saturday.'

'To the Whittles! To the Whittles!' cut in my father dismissively.

At other times my father's interruptions concerned his old chum Parker.

'Parker wasn't invited to that party. It's quite obvious that. I don't know how much of a stink there's been.'

My parents' contact with each other was not always unfriendly but usually remained on a practical level. 'Is there petrol in the tiddler?' asked my mother before setting off on a fishing excursion in the Morris Minor, which my father now used in preference to the Rover, now causing an increasing amount of trouble and expense.

'Will you please remember,' he warned her, 'that there is no spare tyre on that car.'

My father did not treat my mother with the courtesy he showed stray women in London – he would pass a knife to her with its blade pointing forward and he would often bellow 'Sheert up' at her in the rudest possible manner, but beneath this crudeness there lay an element of ancient affection and occasionally there were physical gestures between them which had the effect of making me recoil.

10

During this period I also visited Aunt Peg quite regularly. My aunt's world had grown on me and I would walk down her lane, past weathered red-brick farm buildings populated by wild bantams, with a growing sense of anticipation.

Aunt Peg was often waiting for me outside her front door, a little dog she had been given on a lead at her feet, uncomfortably yanked about as its owner looked this way and that. Peg's slender ungainliness, short-sighted movements and commanding height made her instantly recognisable from a distance, but she did not recognise me until the last moment. As always, she then expected and offered a massive hugging embrace before welcoming me indoors.

The house had not changed a bit – it gave off the familiar odour of cats, herbs, hen food and other not unwholesome smells of childhood holidays in Cumberland. Familiar objects from my grandmother's house floated in the sea of mess. Every shelf, every bit of table and floor space was occupied by some article: blackened buckets of half-cooked potato peelings, baskets of bones, seed potatoes, further bones underfoot, a turd in the dog's dish, two cans of fresh farm milk, a large bread board spread out with filthy cards with which my aunt had been playing Patience before my arrival – or perhaps several weeks earlier.

There was a reason for everything. 'There are bottlenecks in this room, and they are awkward,' Aunt Peg acknowledged, 'but I must keep two beds here.' Behind every arrangement there was a mysterious logic. 'I have to keep the step-ladder in here since I bought the electric kettle,' she explained.

Through an open door I could glimpse her bedroom. It looked like a frightful actress's dressing room, a few of her cleaner clothes on a modern hanging contraption in the corner but many of them entangled in the bedding. The window was permanently open – as at my grandmother's house – to enable the cats to come and go, and the window-sill itself, on which also sat the telephone – so that Aunt Peg could answer it while working in the garden – was covered with earthy footprints.

Another door led to the small high-ceilinged kitchen. Here, buckets of rotting mess blocked the way to an outhouse containing a cheap and highly flexible plastic bath, and behind a noisy metallic sliding door was the facility which Peg somewhat confusingly called 'The Aunt'.

Also beyond the kitchen was the room I slept in, marginally tidier but much damper than the rest of the house, in spite of its open fire. Here hung some of the pastels and engravings which had decorated the staircase at my grandmother's house, many of them now suffering in their new environment, with fungus sprouting beneath the glass. Two beds were also squeezed into this room and kept permanently made up in readiness for the sudden arrival of visitors.

On top of this basic disorder there lay a secondary level of untidy papers, documents, letters, photographs, books on slavery, soil, agriculture. Some of the correspondence was new, some of it dated back half a century. A letter from Buckingham Palace dated 1922 thanking my aunt for the wedding gift her Girl Guide troupe had sent to a royal princess floated on mounds of recently Roneoed County Council minutes and Lake District Planning Board memoranda. New photographs of Tim and Catherine, and Michiko with Toby had already gummed themselves to a message from the London School of Journalism with which Peg had apparently taken a correspondence course in the late 1940s. 'The tone of this article is still a little too dictatorial for the average reader.'

On every visit I came across letters of different vintages. Charming cards from Tim in warm places, notes from Ben when he was working at the hotel school, and a rather grim letter from my mother six years earlier criticising my relationship with Jack Pratt. 'Rather a doubtful friendship. Nobody seems to like him.'

*

The mess in the cottage was made worse by my aunt's method of cleaning it. Every two or three weeks, she thoroughly washed the red sandstone floor of each room with a thick solution of red powder and water. She did this with incredible vigour, getting right down on the floor to do it, explaining, 'You don't get anything like the purchase standing up.'

The trouble with this dark red powder was that it now affected everything. The cats and dog's paws were permanently stained red, so were the legs of the chairs and tables. The cats carried the red dust onto the County Council papers, onto the dishcloths and into the drawers where my aunt kept her silver forks and spoons. Everything was discoloured with it, door handles, the sheets in which I slept and the books I tried to read.

Nothing worried my aunt. She presided over the chaos with a certain aplomb and was rather disconcerted when I tried to tidy up, salvage precious objects or build up the fire. 'I never keep the fire as big as this when I'm alone. I tend to keep a little fire and sit right on top of it,' she said, shifting her leather humpty away from the blaze I had created.

My aunt had not only found happiness. She was perpetually on the crest of a wave. Her health no longer troubled her and she now took her occasional falls in her stride. Her last teeth had been taken out, under chloroform, nearly twenty years earlier and, thanks to my father's advice, she had now been fitted with a decent set of false ones. Her cataract operations – big dramas during our childhood – were now ancient history. 'I had one eye done in a public ward, one eye done in a private ward.' And she appeared to have reached some sort of health plateau of early old age.

She had no wireless or television and kept no calendar or diary that I knew of, but she read the *Daily Telegraph* with care and thus kept abreast of world events, if a few days late. She had no visitors other than her relations and the people at the farm at the end of the lane, who called her 'Miss Peg', and no relationships beyond her County Council ones and the people in the parish, who treated her with the respect due to a descendant of the family which still owned land in the neighbourhood. She was quite content in her isolation and she said – and I believed her – that she was never bored. She played Patience a lot and read and re-read the works of Jane Austen and Trollope. Battered volumes of these favourite authors lay around her bed, all of them flecked with red powder.

She loved the visits of her nephews. Tim would stay one night here on his way to or from a painting assignment in Scotland, sometimes arriving at three in the morning. Edward and his family had stayed, bringing elaborate provisions of their own. Richard had brought some of his family for tea when he rented a holiday cottage in the Lake District, a part of England for which he was experiencing a delayed affection – though Aunt Peg's lifestyle remained entirely beyond the comprehension of Sally, who voiced justifiable fears that the food at the cottage might be unsafe to eat. Peg adored these visits: the family of which she was now rather an untidy appendage was to her the most important family in the world – but her happiness was of a deeper origin and she was apparently quite content to be unvisited for months on end.

*

My aunt's voice sounded as if it had not been used for a while. Though she often spoke to herself it was only in a muttered whisper. When addressing me, her words came out crystal clear, too loud, never fluent, and accompanied by the flicking of her fingers, but carefully enunciated, like the voice of an actress or pantomime star, and sometimes agonisingly upper class. She put her heart and soul into what she was

saying, emphasising each word and punctuating each phrase
with the beginning of a laugh, a dramatic hesitation as if to
check that she was being fully comprehended.

My mother spoke in a mild, gentle murmur, with most of
the corners knocked off. Aunt Peg's voice came from Edwardian
England, and was complimented by her girlish curls, the
ancient pyjamas that she kept on all day, and the man's bright
orange waterproof duffle coat that she wore outdoors.

It was Peg's voice that woke me one morning. She was
working in the cramped scullery beside my room and muttering
to herself as she scrabbled about, uttering the odd mild curse
– 'Oh, plague!' – at some misbehaviour by a cat.

'Did you sleep all right?' I asked, on emerging to find my
aunt bent over some appliance.

'I did,' she replied strangely abstracted. 'But I've just had
an electric shock. I don't know why because it's switched off.'

Our weekends together had no particular structure and the
outside world rarely intruded, the only event of each visit
being the journey across the fields to church on Sunday
morning.

Most of the time, my aunt and I sat talking, playing chess,
or crouching over the fire. Sometimes I remained at the fire
while Peg cooked. She did this slowly, dodging about between
the scullery and the Aga on which sat various bubbling or
hissing skillets, which she would stir with pre-war wooden
spoons. While slipping, sliding or crashing about, she would
occasionally ask me a question.

'And do you like apple in a stew?'

Many of the ingredients she used came from her own garden.
She had a wide range of herbs and put them to the fullest use.
Her thyme had recently died 'of old age' but she had 'any
amount of mint, balm, esterlege, coarse rosemary, bay'.

187

She also ate her own hens, wringing their necks herself, addressing the bird as she did so, 'Calm yourself, my dear. It'll be very quick.'

She was thrifty and self denying, telling me she rarely spent more than a pound when she went to the butcher, and boasting that she had once made a chicken last for thirteen meals. She was also well versed in how long things could be left uneaten without going bad. 'Bacon and ham last well into the summer, providing you keep the bluebottles off.'

Eventually she would serve the meal she had been working on so patiently.

'Here's sauce. And here's gravy. And here's Yorkshire. And here's 'taties.'

Quantities were generous and the absence of meat did not trouble me. Plates and cutlery were an odd mixture. Small plastic cups and saucers, the remnants of a pre-war picnic set, chipped willow-pattern plates. Ancestral silver bearing the family crest was available, but my aunt often preferred to eat with a plastic teaspoon.

The food she served during these weekends included fried apples, sautéed potato chunks, Early Purple vegetable, Cumberland sausages, herb soup, sliced white bread, brawn, black pudding, oatmeal soup, scrag end of mutton. These items were followed by cream and grated apple, semolina and hot chocolate sauce, rhubarb, home-made custard made with eggs laid the same day and eaten with home-made blackcurrant jam, gooseberry cake and often a surprising assortment of cheap fancy buns, including Jacks, a Solway speciality.

To drink there was Brooke Bond tea or the cheapest possible kind of finely powdered coffee, from a rectangular packet.

Our meals were carefully watched by the cats and the dog.

'A pet who begs at meal-times is a perfect curse,' Peg said more than once, but she appeared not to notice when the cats jumped onto the table and clawed at the food she was raising to her mouth. Even a cup of coffee left unattended was liable to get a cat's tongue in it while the awkward new dog looked up enviously from the red sandstone floor.

After meals we would withdraw to the room with the fire, taking with us our coffee and sometimes some cheap chocolate mints. Here we spent many hours together, talking in an open-ended way. 'We've got plenty of coal,' said Aunt Peg. 'I'll have to go and get some more logs soon but not yet.'

Our conversations covered a wide range of familiar topics and included gentle recollections of my brothers as children.

'When Richard and Tim were little boys we all thought Richard was better at painting than Tim!' said Peg, punctuating this dramatic revelation with the beginning of a laugh.

The death of my grandmother had removed the last surviving thorn in my aunt's flesh and she had even adopted a more mellow attitude towards my father.

'I should say your father's a little pleased to have an alderman for his sister-in-law but it stops there.'

These comments were intermingled with comments on the game of chess we might be playing – 'I used my Queen too early. It's always said to be a mistake' – or with plaintive noises from the dog.

'Come and be cuddled,' my aunt said one night and the creature had plunged onto her lap and almost immediately began licking a sore on its mistress's knee. My aunt continued with the game and did not appear to notice what was happening until the dog's teeth came into action. 'She's trying to nibble at the scabs,' she said, finally pushing the dog off.

The cats did not seek these privileges – 'The cat's father

was an odious animal' – but the more friendly of the two was allowed to sleep on her bed.

'The friendly one sleeps on one side and the dog sleeps on the other. So we have three heads on the pillow.'

*

At least twice a day, Peg and I went for a walk together, excursions which were invested with a sense of drama and occasion. 'I must just go to The Aunt. Then I'm ready to come with you.' Sometimes I sauntered out into the lane and waited until she emerged in her orange windjammer, her eyes looking wildly for me.

We would then slowly set off, leaving behind the farmyard atmosphere of her immediate surroundings, with its bantams, hens, crowing cocks, cows on both sides and a fine Hereford bull peering over a fence, and strike out across the parish.

Peg moved slowly but as she slipped and slid and rested her arms on her hips, there was something balletic about her movements.

'I've often done this walk in winter,' she volunteered. 'Looking and listening for the first signs of spring.'

As we ambled along, the dog waddling beside us in an uninterested way, my aunt would talk about the people in the cottages we passed, her voice dropping to a dramatic whisper.

'We know these people quite well but I don't think we'll call as I don't think they'd interest you very much.'

A similar route took us to church on Sunday morning. Again the dog accompanied us and we sat together in the back row, partly because there had been complaints about the dog and partly because my aunt had long ago given up trying to hear the vicar.

After the service, Aunt Peg would vigorously reintroduce

me to the few surviving members of the congregation who knew the family and then there would be a further delay as she attended with surprising care to my grandmother's grave.

Back at the cottage, our lunch would be followed by a last game of chess before my departure, and further pampering from my aunt.

'Do you want sugar in your tea, as you're going on a journey?'

My attempts at conversation remained childish and were treated as such by my aunt. As we walked together to the country bus stop I asked, 'Would the bull eat chocolates, Aunt Peg?'

'I doubt it,' she replied. 'But who in their senses would offer a bull chocolates?'

11

The usual hiss of static preceded my father's voice coming on to the line.

'Oh – er – could I possibly have a room in your flat next week?'

In October 1975 my father's progress down the area steps was slower than before and marked by self-mocking cries. Once indoors, he explained he had torn a calf muscle and soon showed me the leg itself, thin and white and self-bandaged in a rather amateurish way. All health matters fascinated him, especially his own, and he was making the most of his injury.

His mood was more nervous than before, however. For the first time, he expressed worries about the security of the flat – 'You're not frightened of a forced entrance?' – and that night I heard odd rattles from inside his bedroom.

Half an hour after midnight he yelled my name, and when

I tried to open his door I found a pile of metal shoe trees propped against it.

In spite of his injury he began his usual gruelling London schedule next day, explaining at tea-time, 'I lead a painful life with all this walking around but I've got me liver juices running again.'

His presence in London drew me back into the family web. Richard and Tim would come clumping down the area steps with messages for him and he himself was a constant source of gossip, most of it inaccurate, about my siblings and their wives.

'Richard and Sally are going to get a divorce,' he announced solemnly one morning.

I immediately accused him of being spiteful but he remained adamant. 'Sally-told-me-so-last-night,' he said in a triumphant sing-song voice, but I continued to dismiss this as a sour joke.

He also sought information from me. 'When's Catherine going to have puppies?' he asked, and hearing of my recent trip North, he enquired gravely, 'Between you, me and the doorstep, do you think Peg's got long?'

The following night, my father and I were invited to supper at Richard's and I could see no obvious sign of the disharmony to which my father had referred.

Once again the tension was between father and son. 'My God, you must have taken a knock,' said my father referring to the recent stock market falls. 'Of course I haven't had any equities for five years,' he added cheerfully.

'The Manx currency has been devalued too but he doesn't pay tax on it,' Richard muttered. My father continued to gloat throughout the meal and at the end Richard attempted to score a point by asking him to help clear away.

'Would you like to help your father?' he asked me.

My father was rarely invited to undertake domestic work but was complying with his eldest son's suggestion with considerable zest. 'Waterford! Lovely!' he cooed as he carried a glass jug to the sideboard.

'The water goes in the fridge,' said Richard.

'In the fridge?' queried my father, still over-excited.

'Keep it cool,' explained Richard.

When these tasks had been completed, the three of us set off for a pub two streets away.

'I can't walk quickly, Richard, all right?' said my father. 'I can't walk quickly, all right?' A few minutes later he referred to his torn muscle again, 'Do I appear to be walking very, very slowly?'

The main cause of our slow progress was my father's way of stopping to make observations about parked cars – 'That's a very well-kept Rover. Now this here is the ideal car for the island' – and other aspects of the London scene.

When we eventually reached the pub, Richard paid for three half pints.

'How does it compare with the draught on the Isle of Man?' asked Richard, attempting to steer the conversation into an area where my father had often claimed expertise.

Outside there was more lingering while my father studied the pub's menu – 'This is quite good value. You can still eat in London for under a pound.' Richard meanwhile examined the fancy stonework round the doorway. 'Do they chip that out by hand?' he asked, but this appeal to my father's lifelong interest in building matters fell flat.

*

The following night, my father was in a less resilient mood. Instead of taking me to the Ritz, he selected a hotel in Earl's

Court in which he had once stayed before the war. The waitress asked if he had a room number.

'No, we're just "chance", as they say.'

The moment the main course was served, he said, nervously thinking ahead, 'You'll have some coffee. I won't.'

Even in these less expensive places my father worried about the cost of the meal, and his deep-rooted desire not to enjoy himself reasserted itself.

'I spent ten pounds on lunch today,' he said miserably. 'I can see nothing funny about paying these sort of prices. I'm not going to spend that sort of money every night. I'm giving you all a luxury meal tomorrow.'

*

The luxury meal to which he referred had already become an institution, an event that took place on each of his visits to London. What happened was that he went in person to Leadenhall Market early in the day and bought a surprisingly large quantity of smoked salmon and fresh prawns. These would be supplemented with bread and butter and white wine and the whole family would gather at Tim's studio to eat them. The event had been branded The Fish Dinner and was usually a quiet affair. This October, it began unexceptionally, my father sitting low in his chair and rather overawed by his surroundings. 'Tim's painting some quite important people,' he said, eyeing the portraits around the walls.

Catherine and Sally helped serve and my father's mind returned to the Isle of Man and remained focused there. 'You see, there is an upper class on the island,' he said, reverting to his favourite theme.

A moment later he accused Sally of not listening to something he had said.

'I couldn't hear,' she replied. 'I think your mouth was full.'

Suddenly a massive blast shook the building, rattling the portraits on the walls and causing Sally to let out a short scream. My brothers said something about 'the bastards', but my father, who had survived two world wars and lived in London during the Blitz, remained calm and cynical. 'There you are, you see,' he said.

We learnt later that a terrorist bomb had exploded in the letter box at the end of the street.

The following day my father seemed to become more excited about the incident.

'It was the largest explosion I've heard in peacetime,' he told the barman at my local pub.

12

A worse upheaval now hit my family. Sally had not been joking about her marriage. When I called at the studio soon after The Fish Dinner Tim told me that Sally and Richard had parted. After thirteen years of an increasingly sticky marriage, Sally had fallen in love with a married man she had met on a skiing holiday. Richard, said Tim, had not foreseen this possibility and was now on tranquillisers.

I telephoned my eldest brother at his office and he spoke to me in subdued but surprisingly affectionate tones. 'It's not been easy,' he murmured, and went on to say that he was flying to the Isle of Man that weekend to tell them the news.

I followed him a few weeks later to spend Christmas with my parents. I found they had both adjusted to this turn of events. A born pessimist who always expected misfortunes, my father felt reassured by the collapse of Richard's marriage.

My mother, too, seemed untroubled, though she had written a letter to Sally. 'To show an interest,' she explained. 'I didn't want it to look as if we were bored by the whole thing.'

*

Both of them were in fact preoccupied with their own lives. One of my mother's new interests was the big brown Labrador, Honey, who had replaced the last surviving dog, Tommy. My father was still obsessed with his leg injury.

'It's no good expecting me to stride into church,' he said on Christmas morning, 'I'm in a poor way.'

'Come on! We're off!' he said later, clipping himself into the safety belts with which the Morris Minor had now been fitted.

After the service, my father said 'That man sitting behind us is a member of the Junior Carlton Club.' Then he suddenly stopped the car outside a council house and went inside with a bottle of sherry. An hour later, my mother served up the usual turkey platter and my father let out a long, patronising and sarcastic, 'Ooooooh!', perhaps embarrassed to be so well provided for. He then raced through the dish and began heckling as I filled my mother's wine glass to the brim. 'Now then, plum pudding,' he said with a blob of bread sauce still on his chin.

He slowed down a bit when he reached the port stage, burying his head in the sideboard and saying 'Now this is very sad. Some of the port glasses have evidently been broken.'

'Oh, no, they haven't,' came my mother's voice from the kitchen.

The glasses were then found and my father solemnly poured some Old Bismarck port into a decanter, remarking as he did so, 'This is the top stuff.'

'Thank you,' he said as I then stretched out to help myself. 'I'll test it first.'

He eventually filled my glass but moved the decanter to his side of the table beyond my reach. 'Now, William, you've had your ration,' and he soon made a performance of putting the decanter into the cupboard, addressing it as he did so. 'Bye bye. See you again in the spring.'

Later that afternoon the new Labrador started barking wildly when we all stood up for the National Anthem introducing the Queen's Speech.

'Yes, Honey, we've all gone mad,' said my mother, but she remained upright and solemn-faced.

'Haven't we had enough television?' said my father an hour later.

'It's Christmas Day, Father,' I replied.

'You want to cut down on Christmas Day,' he said. 'Look, we're on a farm. We're not in Cobham.' Then something on the screen caught his attention. 'That chap's a socialist, if you didn't know.'

Both my parents now seemed to shrink from national events. My mother was more interested in a butterfly she had found in the middle of winter.

'It was drowning in the soup. I thought whatever's that? I picked it out with a spoon and it flew away.'

My father's level of talk was also on a humbler level. One of his main sources of gossip was the woman living in a cottage at the end of the drive – 'Oh, d'you know what Miss Giddy told me about Mr Moores?' He now recoiled from some of the more interesting people on the island. 'They bore me, frankly, he said of a young couple who had been particularly friendly and hospitable to them. They are rackety people.'

He preferred the company of retired members of the armed services. 'Tonight,' he said, 'we have one of the most distinguished airmen of the last war coming to this house. Air

Marshal,' he paused and said with emphasis, 'not Air Vice-Marshal. Air Marshal,' he paused again, 'Sir Talbot Robertson.'

'What are you offering him to drink?' asked my mother.

'The lot,' replied my father.

Then he turned to me, 'You'll have to make yourself rather scarce.'

'I'm warning you, William,' he said later. 'This is a very small island. No funny stuff tonight.'

The matter of Richard's marriage was hardly referred to – and then only in an oblique way. One effect of the crisis was to make my father heap even more praise on his other English daughter-in-law.

'Catherine is a wonderful person,' he said in unctuous tones.

He also brooded over the fact that Sally had screamed after the bomb blast and claimed that this indicated an unstable disposition. 'I should have smacked her across the face. Like this,' he said clapping his hands together in different directions, and making the dog bark.

On a more playful note my father said, 'Has Richard been anywhere near Friends House or Westminster Meeting since this matter?'

13

A much graver and sadder affair was soon to transfix my father's attention. Long ago, before my teens, one of my brothers had mentioned that my mother had had an operation for cancer. Too young to comprehend this information, I was merely curious in the manner of a child and must have forgotten about it.

Since that day, at least twenty years earlier, my mother's

health had not presented any problems that I knew of. Certainly, my mother had never mentioned anything and my father's occasional speeches about his wife's health were so obliquely worded as to mean nothing to me.

Now in the spring of 1976 my father told me in the grimmest possible manner that my mother had had a repetition of 'her trouble'. She did not wish to talk about it, he explained, and from then on my father was the only source of information about the illness. It was still difficult to believe everything he said or to extract straightforward information from him.

When he met me at Douglas dock for the first time since this disclosure I found him almost delirious. During the whole journey home he talked about my mother's illness, or rather its consequences for him. At this stage his main area of concern seemed to be the cost of the treatment and of a hospital room.

'That'll come off your inheritance,' he said.

'What an absolutely ghastly remark,' I replied.

'No, no, no,' continued my father, completely unabashed and stubbornly missing the point. 'It doesn't affect me. I receive a legacy.'

When we reached the house, he became more subdued and I found my mother carrying on as before, quite unchanged and perhaps in rather better form than usual.

So it was to continue. During the months ahead, my mother became calmer and calmer while my father became more and more nervous and desperate. 'He wants to get the last ounce of work out of her,' commented Aunt Peg; but instead of retreating into domestic routine, my mother struck out as never before. In the baking summer of 1976 she at last accepted a long-standing invitation to visit Edward and Michiko in Japan. My father started by being hostile to this idea but eventually became excited about it.

'It's the sensation of the whole Northern Plain that you're going,' he said with real awe, and was even more perturbed when he learnt that Edward was providing my mother with first-class air tickets.

'Well, of course,' he said, after he had thought about it. 'He's got the money to do it. The bank's simply shovelling money into his pockets.'

*

My mother was away for three weeks. My father used the time to tour familiar golf courses and visit me again in London. Soon after my mother's return, I received another letter from him.

'After coming back from Japan, your mother is having trouble again and Dr Morris had her x-rayed today. Next week we shall know, and you will be told, whether the plate shows any spread of the trouble.'

My father's letters struck a reasonable note, but in person he remained hysterical. One way or another, however, it became clear that my mother's illness was worsening.

A few weeks after her return from Japan, she began a course of weekly injections. She did not talk about the side-effects of this treatment or of the illness itself. She became increasingly at ease with herself. The forlornness that I had noticed for years lifted and a serenity took its place. She became cosier, gentler, more companionable, more tolerant, more fragile but less broken by domestic drudgery.

In contrast, my father cut a more and more miserable figure in his heavy clothing, frayed waistcoat, now uncomfortably combined with a protruding 'batik' tie given to him by Michiko for his sixty-eighth birthday, short cheap socks and brown plimsolls imprinted with the words 'For Speed And Action'.

Instead of being gentle with my mother, he was either

patronising or officious. My mother had only to clear her throat for him to say, quick as a flash, 'When is your next injection, Mummy?' The challenge of the illness had brought out the worst in him. He was beside himself with anxiety and selfishness. He demanded attention the whole time, even to the extent of grabbing a book I was reading out of my hands. He made constant references to the illness – 'When do you take your medicine, Mummy?' 'When it's necessary' – and constantly re-calculated my mother's chances of surviving.

'She'd love to live to see you married.'

My mother responded to all this with unfailing politeness, but my father never gave up pestering her and seemed to do his utmost to make the side-effects of her treatment sound as unpleasant as possible. He also spoke relentlessly of the cost of the illness, announcing 'the good news' at one junction that a less expensive form of treatment was now being used.

'Mercifully. For you. Not me.'

14

The sad drama of my mother's illness eclipsed Richard's troubles. In fact, my eldest brother had only remained on tranquillisers for a few weeks. He was soon fit and well, hardened by the experience, and able to cope with the upheaval. The divorce pressed ahead, the property was divided, Sally kept the children and quickly remarried, but there was little acrimony. Richard moved into a rented flat in Knightsbridge while he looked around for a more permanent home for himself.

I saw more of him than before. We had lunch together occasionally at the West End club he had recently joined, and he would sometimes call at my basement. He now owned a motorbike and would chain this to the railings and come down the area steps carrying his shiny black helmet.

I also visited him at his rented flat. One weekend I found his whole family assembled there, including Sally. While the children laughed, shrieked – 'You made a fart!' – and did handstands on the sofa, Richard's ex-wife questioned him closely about the flat he had decided to buy on Royal Hospital Road.

'How many rooms has it got?'

Richard was cheerfully submitting to the inquisition and said, 'Shall I draw you a little map?' As he explained his new home Sally responded with a mixture of envy and curiosity and a certain maternal tone.

'That's a window seat by the way.'

'Gosh, how lovely.'

'That's a working fireplace.'

'Gosh, how amazing. Sounds smashing. Your own flat. It's all one big room is it?'

Richard pressed on, ignoring some of her questions.

'I'll put the grandfather clock there and I'm going to put my desk there and my filing cabinet and things.'

'Nice kitchen, is it?'

'It's OK.'

'Where will you park? It's difficult to park, isn't it?'

'I want to find a big rug,' he said.

'But surely, Daddy,' piped up a child, 'you've got lots of carpets. You've got at least five.'

'I need two runners,' he insisted. 'Those long things. Do you remember that long carpet we had in the hall? I'm on Sotheby's list for carpets. I've subscribed just for rugs.'

'You shouldn't have bought that flat,' said another child. 'I liked the one next to the school.'

15

My mother was not obviously ill or physically changed by her illness and if it had not been for my father's increasingly lugubrious commentary on the state of his wife's health, one might have forgotten about it. My mother remained active. The following spring, she visited London, stayed in Richard's new flat and she and I had lunch together in a restaurant in Chelsea.

I was touched by the simplicity of her clothes and her unfamiliarity with London. Several times on the street she stumbled, though she was not short-sighted. When we arrived at the restaurant, the waitress asked if we would like an aperitif. My mother was unfamiliar with this word but she accepted a Dubonnet and drank her share of the wine I ordered later. Throughout the meal she remained oriented towards the Isle of Man and the minutiae of daily life there.

'We bought four hens for the pot for twenty-five pee each,' she began one anecdote. 'One was dead in the crate when it arrived. We gave that to the dog. One was lame with a ball of muck on its foot. We had to soak it off with hot water. Tim helped. We ate one. It was perfectly good with parsley sauce. One just ailed and died. We buried it. The rats have already dug it up.'

Though frail and shy, my mother seemed happier than many of the women I met in London and certainly happier than my father who, she reported, now spent a lot of his time sitting gazing into the fire.

*

My visits to the Isle of Man continued. One weekend I told my mother that I had obtained a contract to write a book.

She was interested but did not pepper me with questions about it and after a while said, 'Let's change the subject.'

Later, we sat together in deckchairs outside the front door the big Labrador wallowing amiably beside us.

'You can sit here doing nothing,' said my mother. 'You couldn't inside the house. Oh, sun, please come out. We're not warm enough without you. I don't trust the afternoon. The clouds are rather rolling up.'

A thin Manx cat joined the party, threading itself between two wooden tubs of nasturtiums.

'We've even got Catty. Whom I'm not fond of, I'm afraid.'

The only figure who would not relax was my father. He strode about, crunching the gravel, a piece of shirt protruding from his fly buttons, looking for something to do. Approaching us he said, 'Oh by the way, those tubs are going . . . I'm having . . . concrete . . .'

My mother's calmness seemed to increase his agony. Even the new dog he handled with a strange jerkiness and a mockery of affection. 'Oh he's a good dog,' he crooned, getting the animal's gender wrong, then starting to shout coarsely, 'Dog! Dog! Doggy dog! Dog!'

Back in the house my father continued to persecute the animal, and when he found the dog's plate of food uneaten he said, 'Hello, he's off-colour.'

Another cause for my father's concern was the lady who lived in the cottage at the end of the drive. Miss Giddy and my father had now fallen out and my father had begun to question her sanity.

'I think she's been in a mental hospital,' he said.

'How on earth do you pick up these things?' I asked.

'Because I think she's been the subject of proceedings,' he said, and he was not prepared to let the matter rest.

'I've got to speak to the vicar about it. Of all people. Now I want this room to myself. Or I must go to another room. I'm just ringing up this chap for a moment.'

He breathed heavily through his nostrils as he consulted the telephone directory.

'Good morning, John. Or rather, good afternoon, John,' he began. 'Now we enjoyed yesterday's evensong very much. May I talk business? What about Miss Giddy? I don't know whether she is taking pills. Is it wise to make peace with someone who is fairly obviously an ex-mental patient? Or should have been? All this has been reported to the police of course. It had to be.'

While this was going on, my mother and I entertained each other by making cocktails, Gin Fizz, White Ladies, and other concoctions from an old recipe book, laughing over them and sipping and spilling them together. In recent months my mother had started keeping her own stock of drinks in the back kitchen and there was no shortage of ingredients.

This rare, companionable session ended suddenly when my father re-entered the kitchen.

'When is your boat?' he asked fiercely.

*

About two months later, my mother became seriously ill. In the late summer of 1977, shortly after her sixty-seventh birthday, she was taken to hospital. A quick consultation between my brothers and me took place and it was agreed that Tim should fly to the island at once and that I should take over from him in two or three days' time.

That evening, Tim telephoned me from the island to say that my mother was now heavily sedated and delirious.

'Is there any hope?' I asked.

'I should have thought not,' he said. 'The nurse said "Shall I ring you if anything happens in the night?"'

He went on to say that my father was 'surprisingly chirpy', but when he rang the next day to say that my mother's condition was unchanged he added that he was now having 'flaming rows' with my father, who was even trying to prevent him using the telephone.

'I'm no good at vegetables,' Tim added, 'I don't know what's edible here.'

The following day I telephoned the island and the telephone was answered by an unfamiliar male voice.

'Pop's out somewhere,' said the stranger. 'Timothy left this morning.'

When I eventually got my father, he said tersely, 'When are you coming? I've doubled the help,' and I agreed to fly there the next morning.

That night I had another consultation with Tim and Richard at the studio. Richard told me to be prepared to be my father's verbal punchbag. Tim warned me that my father only spoke normally for a few minutes a day and advised me, 'Let him prattle on about the will.'

*

I was met at the airport by the man who had answered the telephone at the house. He was the local taxi-driver, a small, sandy-haired man of Welsh origin, whose car smelt of after-shave and air freshener. He knew everyone on the island and waved and hooted frequently as we drove northwards.

I found my father in an appalling state, trailing around the house in his dressing-gown, carrying my mother's handbag. Later, he donned his cap and mackintosh and wandered about so blinkered by his own misery that he twice barged straight into me.

'Sorry,' I said automatically when our bodies collided.

He rode roughshod over my own grief, seemed as unaware as ever of my mother's personality and did not once mention the idea of Heaven. Most of his outpourings concerned financial arrangements and his desire to save himself small sums. I learnt, for example, that he had refused to telephone Edward, now stationed in Hong Kong, but had economised by placing a call to the London branch of Edward's bank and asked them to contact his son.

'The Chinaman Will Pay,' he gleefully repeated.

Not only did he prattle on about the will, he was also talking a great deal about the likely cost of the funeral, boasting that he was already haggling with various funeral directors 'for the sake of my sons' – and recalling that he had done just the same on his own mother's death thirty years earlier.

'I beat the ring and went to the Co-op.'

For the sake of peace, I found myself subscribing with murmurs of approval.

He also talked of remarriage. He had mentioned this subject often over the years and I had laughed it off, but now I found myself expressing encouragement as he clung defiantly to this hope, justifying it by repeating more than once, 'I am not a homosexualist. I am not a homosexualist.' He more or less indicated that he had set his sights on Veronica Bobbin, one of the Bobbin sisters who lived at Glen Doon on the edge of the Northern Plain. He was still talking along these lines when he drove me to the hospital to visit my mother. My father had suggested that I entered the room alone. It was the first time I had ever seen my mother in hospital and the first time that my mother had ever looked old. She lay awake, her face desperately thin, toothless, her eyes large and staring, but not at me. She spoke my name and I found her hand under the bedclothes but after a few moments she withdrew it and I did not try to find it again. She looked exhausted and frightened yet had an unearthly dignity and grace, an Oriental look that Tim had pointed out a long time ago now quite pronounced. I said a few useless sentences, she spoke several words I could not understand. Then a nurse entered and tried to feed her with an odd spouted vessel, calling her 'Poppet' as she did so.

'Come along, Poppet,' said the nurse but soon my mother's head went sideways onto the pillow.

A small side table was crowded with flowers that she could not see or appreciate.

Suddenly my father burst into the room. He was still wearing his mackintosh and the hem of this garment caught on the temperature chart at the end of my mother's bed, bringing it clattering to the floor.

'Well, there you are,' he said, protecting himself against any emotion he might feel by a dull matter-of-factness. He did not go close to the bed, let alone sit beside it in case my mother had a lucid moment.

As we drove home, my father had another subject on his lips. One of the neighbours. Mrs Whittle, was being, he considered, far too attentive to my mother, visiting the hospital far too often and making what my father called 'emotional scenes'.

'I've told her she must ask Sister before she goes in again.'

He did not leave this subject alone and soon went so far as to describe this well-meaning neighbour as 'a lesbian type', backing up this calumny by saying, 'Your mother knew what it was all in aid of,' and as so often before attributing to my mother a snobbishness she did not begin to possess.

'Your mother cannot stand that treacly Birmingham accent.'

This hostility to Mrs Whittle soon reached a climax – 'She needs her trousers pulling down and given a bloody good hiding – and I'd like to do it!' – but eventually this petered out. That night my father became relatively normal, offering cigars and port and sitting beside the fire I had lit. The big fat Labrador, which had quickly transferred her affections to him, lay at his feet.

'Dog is well,' he remarked obliquely. 'He's not concerned with matters.

At the end of the evening, my father surprised me by telephoning Aunt Peg and giving her a coarse account of my mother in hospital – 'head back, eyes open, teeth out' – but added more poetically that my mother was now 'sailing peacefully out of life'.

Thus the visit continued. My father swung between madness and mellowness. I took over the kitchen and my father quickly slipped into treating me as his new servant. I drifted sadly about the house and garden. I wept when I found the vegetable plot my mother had looked after so carefully was already overgrown with weeds. In the back kitchen I wept again when I came upon the store of whisky and gin that my mother had begun to keep only a few months earlier and I immediately made extravagant use of it.

Twice a day my father drove me in the Morris Minor to the hospital where my mother slept in a resigned but not entirely peaceful way, more like an animal caught in a trap, occasionally breaking through into a dazed, agonised consciousness. The last time I saw her, one of her feet made a powerful kick under the blankets.

*

After three days I returned to London, leaving my father on his own for twenty-four hours before Richard took my place. The crisis had brought us brothers closer together and on the night of my return we all met again in Tim's studio, mainly to discuss my father's future.

'There could be another twenty-five years in him,' said Richard grimly.

'Our problems have not even begun,' said Tim.

Catherine was now pregnant and she tactfully fell asleep during this discussion which also covered the possibility of my father's remarriage. We had all met Veronica Bobbin and Richard was sufficiently brainwashed by my father's talk about this lady to remark, 'I'd be quite proud of her as a stepmother.'

*

It was five days later, during Tim's second stint on the island, that my mother died. Tim broke the news to me, and to various other relations, and the following morning I telephoned my father and found him very calm and speaking of 'a great relief'. He was now busy with the legal work and general correspondence connected with my mother's death and he added more breezily, 'I'm now in the position of quite a hard-pressed junior executive.'

We were all together on the island for the funeral, including Aunt Peg and Edward. The latter was able to combine the visit with business in London and he had arrived at my basement at 8.15 in the morning, spent two hours on the telephone and then gone off to a day packed with impromptu meetings.

My father was in top form at the funeral, wearing his darkest and smartest suit, a stiff white collar, watch chain, and for the first time in years, his bowler hat, a sartorial combination which momentarily reinstated him as the dandified figure who had visited us at boarding school. The church was crowded. I stood beside Aunt Peg and held her hand at one moment, choking back tears.

Afterwards there was a small gathering at the house. My father remained on the crest of a wave, delighted to have his four surviving sons around him for the first time for eight years, carrying with it the opportunity to boss us all around again.

'I will not have funeral drinking,' he said at one point in the proceedings. 'So cut it out!'

16

We all went our separate ways leaving my father alone without too much anxiety. There was little we could do but wait and see how he managed.

Within a week of the funeral, my father telephoned me and said, 'The penny's dropped,' but a few weeks later he visited London briefly and seemed quite pleased with his solitariness.

'And you lunch with whom, Father?' I asked, prodding him one morning with my bare foot.

'I shan't lunch with anyone,' he replied loftily. 'I shall just have a scrap meal up at a bar.'

He returned later, boasting, 'I have never been to the City before, wearing flannel trousers and a brown slouch hat,' and bragging about a buxom blonde who had chatted him up in a pub. 'Not being a homosexualist, I was naturally very interested,' he said.

He was in perky, insolent form – 'Why don't you put yourself down for a council flat?' – and even Tim came in for jocular criticism.

'Tim has been told to reduce his overdraft. He must paint more pictures.'

*

A few days later he was back on the island alone and when I telephoned him there I found him less resilient.

'Mr Sweet says it'll cost me fifty pounds a week to have a housekeeper,' he said.

Sighs and silence followed and I guessed – correctly as it turned out – that Veronica Bobbin had quickly made it clear she was not interested in marrying him.

'I wouldn't be surprised if Father threw himself off Ramsey pier,' said Tim. But when he and Catherine went over to the island in November they came back with a rosy report that my father was in robust health, well looked after by two daily women and with a fridge full of fillet steak.

The ups and downs continued. Soon after Tim's cheerful account there came the first evidence that my father was not managing on his own.

At the beginning of December, he telephoned me, weighed down with self-pity, saying that he had summoned the police in the middle of the previous night, believing that there was a man on the roof of the house.

'I was examined by the police surgeon to make sure I wan't taking too many drugs. Of course it would be a very serious matter for the doctors if I was.'

*

On Christmas Eve, I flew to the Isle of Man and was met at the airport by the taxi driver, now dressed in waterproof shoes and a cap. During the journey north he chattered about everyone we passed and when we eventually pulled into my father's driveway, he said in a loud voice, 'Welcome home!'

The big Labrador came out of the house first and made a fuss over the taxi driver.

'D'you think I'm bootiful?' said the man. 'D'you think I'm bootiful?'

I was the only member of the family present that Christmas and during the next four days I played the role my mother had played, ministering to my father and managing the house. My mother's spirit lived on, the house was still full of her arrangements, though already a little tidier. The extra help my father had recruited had applied herself to the family furniture and it had begun to shine as it had not for years.

I took over the kitchen during my stay and looked after the dog and cat.

The latter animal, the poor tail-less creature that no one loved, now seemed unwell and my father was annoyed when he found I had left a small heater on in the kitchen to keep it warm during the night. 'The cat'll cost you a hundred a year if you do things like that,' he said, turning it off.

My father had informed me on the telephone that a turkey had been delivered and, on the morning of Christmas Day, I set about cooking this with the help of one of my mother's recipe books. Eventually I opened the hatch through to the room where my father sat inactive and said, 'It's five minutes to go, Father. Then we're going to sit down to lunch together. No walking off into the garden, do you hear?'

Throughout his marriage, my father had shrunk from the intimacy of shared meals and had to be constrained into eating at the same time as other people. Now, true to form, he had immediately sprung into action and had gone upstairs, wrenching open a drawer in his bedroom.

213

Thinking for a moment that he might be looking for paper with which to wrap a present for me, I held back. I had already told him I wanted a pair of galoshes for Christmas, and since galoshes were things he respected – he had never worn gumboots in his life – I wondered if he might be wrapping up a pair at that moment.

I was mistaken. He was putting on a pair of long pants – as I could see only too clearly when he reappeared with their bottoms peeping out at his ankles.

At last I placed a plate of turkey and some of its accompaniments in front of him.

'On my death, fifty thousand. All right?' he said in gratitude.

He had opened some wine several hours earlier, but as soon as I had a second glass, he grabbed the bottle back.

'Right. Now, I'm corking it up, 'nkyou,' he said, truncating the last word in the manner of an old-fashioned bus conductor.

After lunch he opened my present and the presents I had brought from my brothers. I waited in vain for the galoshes, but he eventually revealed that he had at least ordered a pair for me. He also boasted that he had not given a gift to any of his grandchildren.

'Look, I'm giving them eight or nine thousand each. So I don't think it matters very much, does it? Honestly?'

Later we sat together beside the fire and my father brooded about himself and his extended family, while the big Labrador Honey raised bloodshot eyes at us. My father was up to all his old tricks, denigrating and elevating his sons, one by one.

'Richard is hoping for an introduction through Catherine to someone he can marry'; 'Tim's got there, hasn't he? But you haven't, old chap'; 'How's your girl friend? The one Tim said you met at the Southwaters' dance?'; 'You must get approaches from homos the whole time, a young man living alone'; 'You're thirty-two next year', and remarks along these lines eventually gave way to a monologue about himself.

He delivered this in a doleful voice with many clearings of the throat. His talk that afternoon began with his neighbour Miss Bobbin, on whom he had placed such high hopes and who had so quickly rebuffed him and with whom he was not even now on friendly terms.

'I'm just waiting to sling a writ against Veronica!' he said.

The monologue led up to a gloomy description of his current existence and stressed his need to remarry.

'I can't have affairs. Living here as the local squire.'

'The local squire?'

'Well, who else is there?'

These thoughts were finally punctuated by a strangely earthy and commonplace remark, largely rhetorical.

'So you've got the answer there, haven't you, chum?'

*

At half past three my father closed the curtains, though it was still light outside, and announced that he had a cold, which he was certain I would soon catch.

'I'm sorry for you in London with it,' he said as he inspected the Christmas cards, several of which were addressed to both my parents, by those ignorant of my mother's death.

'Did we have more last year, do you think?' he asked and he soon began patiently counting. 'Thirty-three, thirty-four . . . forty-six, forty-seven, forty-eight . . . We've got about seventy, sixty-five or seventy.'

Later I tried to watch a television variety show. Hearing the orchestra strike up, he remarked, 'Lovely, lovely noises,' but he soon began counting again, this time the figures on his bank statements and cheque stubs which lay littered across his lap.

While I attempted to listen to a comedian telling a joke, my father rustled his bank statements and began counting in a louder voice.

'Fifty-one. Fifty-six. And three. Fifty-nine. Look. Would you mind turning it off? It's Christmas Day. A religious day.'

He did not attend to the television until the News, and when finally the lady newscaster wished us all a Happy Christmas, my father said, 'She's drunk.'

*

I remained on the island for several days, during which my father's mood fluctuated. Part of the time he was in fighting form, delighted to have a son to push around and mock.

'Where's my coffee?' he shouted crudely and an hour later, finding me tackling a blocked sink, sneered, 'You'll never do it,' just as I was succeeding in this task.

Sooner or later, he lost his temper and accused me of stealing my mother's engagement ring. At first I thought this was a joke and tried to laugh it off, but soon he was questioning me intently, like a policeman or the public prosecutor he had once been.

On my last evening, he was back to normal, dangling a dirty handkerchief in front of Honey. 'I'm trying to infect the dog with my cold but there's no sign of it yet.'

Absent from the scene was the stub-tailed cat. It had disappeared on Christmas Day and when four days later I finally got into the taxi that was to take me back to the airport, its miserable saucer of food still sat outside the back door, uneaten and now diluted with rainwater.

17

'I miss your mother frightfully. Frightfully.'

I did not doubt this but noticed that Aunt Peg was less brought down by my mother's death than I might have expected. In fact, she now surprised me by coming to London, her first visit since Tim's wedding.

Richard had at last become an admirer of Aunt Peg, hailing her as a 'Bloomsbury' character, and inviting her to stay in his new flat. It was here that I visited her one afternoon in his absence. Peg had now passed her seventieth birthday and cut a magnificent figure – tall, gaunt, still golden-haired, though less at ease in the rather commonplace rayon suit instead of the button-fronted combination pyjamas she usually wore in her cottage. The flat, with its modern facilities, may also have unnerved her.

Peg's voice remained as confident as ever, and as always she concentrated totally on what she was saying even to the extent of ignoring the coffee cup that she sent flying. We soon found our conversational territory and she chatted on about her various interests with gusto.

'I love the country till it hurts,' she said, 'but I'm quite happy in a town.'

'You're enjoying your seventies?' I asked.

'Thoroughly.'

One reason for her visit to London was to see Tim's twins. Catherine had given birth to two baby girls at the beginning of March and they were now installed in the flat in which I had once lived below my brother's studio.

'Catherine is a marvellous person, isn't she?' I said.

'Yes,' said Peg, 'and I thought Sally was too.'

It was only when we began to talk about my father that a new note entered my aunt's voice. She no longer hated her brother-in-law but spoke about him with a certain detachment. When I pressed her to describe the circumstances in which he and my mother had first met, she sounded condescending about him.

'He was The Man Who Lived In The Crown Hotel and that was all we knew about him,' she said.

It was at a dance at the hotel, near Carlisle – where my father had lived for several months during the mid-1930s – at a subscription dance to raise money for the local hospital that my parents had first met.

'The Infirmary Ball counted particularly as a County occasion,' explained Aunt Peg. 'You know the old meaning of that word? But, er, anyone could buy tickets . . . And as he was living there . . . He went up to Tom Little and said "Do introduce me to that charming girl in green" . . . Then he started asking her out to walk at weekends . . . Of course, your mother was far more popular than I was with men. I mean, that was taken as read.'

18

A brand new chapter now opened in my father's life. At the age of seventy-one, he fell in love with a Wiltshire widow named June.

As so often with matters involving my father, one was wholly dependent on his version of events and in fact it was several months before I learnt how this episode had begun.

It then became the subject of a slow, undulating and polished monologue to which each of his sons was subjected in rotation.

My first turn came during a visit to the Isle of Man in the summer. Hitherto, he had merely dropped hints. At Easter he had remarked perkily, 'This may be the last time you stay here with just me. Next time there may be someone else here.'

Now he told me the full story.

'June has come into my life since January,' he began in sombre voice and went on to describe how a chance Christmas card from this old Wiltshire acquaintance had started him off on a whole new marriage tack.

'She sent me a delightful Christmas card, which was of course addressed to both of us. I telephoned her in January and told her what had happened. She told me that she was carrying on farming on the Dockington estate outside Bath and it was obvious that she very much wanted me to come and see her next time I was down in Wilt-char.' He pronounced the last word as might a music hall squire.

By the time of my summer visit, my father was in a frenzy about his relationship with June.

'I would like to marry her,' he said flatly, 'and – you may be surprised to hear this – for physical reasons.'

His desires and calculations were still infinitely hypothetical, however, as the lady in question was apparently undecided about the idea.

At the first opportunity, I opened my father's filing cabinet and soon found a number of letters from June, in a file discreetly marked 'Dockington', next to one marked 'Dog'. The letters were full of affectionate phrases – several of them began 'My Dear Manxman' – but as far as I could make out they all firmly turned down his proposals. For some reason, these rejections were couched so gracefully that my father had misunderstood them and the possibility of marriage to this lady remained constantly on his mind and excluded all references to other matters, especially to my mother, for whom he had as yet not expressed any sentiment at all. The only reference he made to his late wife was: 'June's family wouldn't have had anything to do with your mother's family a hundred years ago.'

He also used the friendship as a further stick with which to beat his eldest son. 'June would immediately weigh him up as bogus. It's done by sheer acting, Richard's work, not real skill like working out a long Chancery case.'

He had fun, too, speculating about the effect that marriage to June would have on his old adversary Veronica Bobbin. 'I'd like to see a first-class stand-up row between June and Veronica,' he said.

'I think you're going to find June a delightful addition to the family,' he said; but the financial aspects of the decision were what really obsessed him and were now tackled from every angle and at every hour of the night and day.

'The Dockington estate is four hundred acres,' he said out of the blue. 'That makes it worth around seven hundred thousand.'

Rumours of the romance had also reached the big ears of my father's tame taxi-driver, who remarked as he drove me to the airport at the end of my visit, 'Dad needs a snazzier car if he wants to go a-courting.

*

A few weeks later, my father's life was over-shadowed by a visit from his old friend Bobbie and for almost a week there was a strange silence from the island. He then telephoned me and said he had had the worst week of his life, during which his old girlfriend had drunk eighteen half-bottles of vodka.

'Bobbie must never stay here again,' he said in a lifeless voice.

A few days later, Richard telephoned me to say that my father had suffered a mild stroke. He had been informed by one of the cleaning ladies that her boss had taken to his bed and was eating little. 'It's in his mind,' the cleaning lady had added.

Fears that my father was cracking up were unfounded. He was soon up and about and on the telephone again to his sons. 'I haven't had a black-out,' he told me, 'more of a white-out'. He also added cheerfully, 'Mrs Whittle's been to see me.'

His doctor had prescribed him a mild anti-depressant which had the effect of making him sound madly elated and rather forgetful. When I made a passing reference to 'Dockington' – never off his lips during my last visit to the island – he said sharply. 'How the devil do you know that name?'

*

In the autumn my father visited London again. His moods were affected by every little twist and turn in his relationship with June – and the anxiety had taken its toll.

He had lost weight and his generously cut waistcoat, grey flannels and Prince of Wales check coat hung even looser on him. He also seemed to have lost his touch with inferiors. When he wished a passing policeman good morning, he was met with barely a grunt of acknowledgment.

In the pub where we had lunch, his face wore an expression of untold misery which was underlined by his humble request to the waitress – 'Piece of bread, please.' This was followed by the gloomy observation, 'This isn't as good as I could do myself,' and finally by, 'The muck I eat in London!'

Back in my basement, he was in better form, disclosing with a mischievous twinkle that his doctor had now told him to masturbate. He let this revelation sink in, then raised a reproving finger and added, 'But not too much!'

His mood improved. He coughed confidently, speculated again about Richard's relationship with Black – 'The friendship was a questionable one. I won't say further than that' – and generally made his presence felt. He shouted about my forthcoming thirty-second birthday, spoke less respectfully of my landlady – 'How's the old bag upstairs?' – and farted as he walked along to the bathroom, wedging its door shut and shooting the bolt home loudly. Our relationship was back to its normal jokiness for a while.

When I tapped on the bathroom door, my father said, 'What do you want?'

'I don't know, Father.'

'I know what you want. What you want is a wife,' came from within.

His own desire for a wife remained paramount and was more desperate than my own. June was still the focus of his attention, but his comments on the possible marriage had become more and more concerned with the financial aspects of any liaison.

'She feels that with her own farm income and some unearned income, we would be well off compared with the majority of English people, but if I went down there my family would have to pay the estate duty on my death. And if she died before me I'd be horribly badly off and in a very difficult position about marrying again. She doesn't lose a penny by marrying me but I might find myself in the hands of a very much stronger character than myself.'

Now, at last, he began to talk about my mother, almost for the first time since her death.

'Your mother had a character that was never put on the table,' he began with strange detachment. 'If it was there, it was shielded from me and everybody else. On the other hand, she seemed to control five boys quite well, didn't she? She wouldn't stand much rot really. I mean we never had anything like Tim or Edward going to the pub and coming back roaring drunk. If anything like that happened it was never in the presence of your mother. She was able to keep everybody in order. Somehow or other.'

The strain of these monologues, and the high element of wishful thinking about June, drove me out of my own flat. His presence cut me off from my friends and I became temporarily as isolated as him. While perambulating the neighbourhood in these circumstances, I chanced to see my father on a road island near South Kensington Station. He looked sad and lost.

A few days later, he returned to the Isle of Man and promptly telephoned me.

'One person rang up while I was away. One person. Mrs Quiggin did not take his name.'

19

As my father's life went into a decline, his sons and grand-children flourished. Tim's twins began to crawl around the floor of his studio, chased by Catherine. Tim travelled again to far-off places with an extraordinary calm and unfussed invulnerability which showed in his work. Calm little land-scapes executed in between commissioned portraits temporarily adorned the walls of his studio before hanging briefly in the little Belgravia gallery where he held regular shows. His fame spread mainly by word of mouth.

'Do you have a brother called Tim?' people asked on learning my name and then, 'I recognised the family resemblance.'

I would report these encounters to Tim but he was never

particularly interested, indeed he sometimes claimed to have no knowledge of the person in question.

'More fools know Tom Fool than Tom Fool knows,' he said, yet in his subtle way he gossiped much of the time and was particularly communicative when discussing Richard's activities.

And Richard had become a rich source of gossip. Since the break-up of his marriage he had become a philanderer. According to Tim, he had slept with the lady from whom he had bought his flat – and at least three others in as many months. Now he had fallen in love with a young American actress.

'Which would you prefer as a sister-in-law?' asked Tim.

Richard had changed considerably during the last two years. While Tim, Edward and I plodded on as before, Richard was undergoing the long-awaited identity crisis. He had become a modern man. The tweeds and grey flannels and brogues, a painful echo of my father's wardrobe, had at last been discarded in favour of linen suits and the odd leather jacket. His hair, for years smacked down as he had done it in the army, now fluffed up into a cheerful quiff. Richard wore spectacles now but these too were lightly framed and daringly coloured.

This transformation had gone down well with everyone except my father – 'Those tiny little tight trousers. Those awful spectacles' – and was matched by a psychological change.

The American actress had in fact encouraged him to take an interest in psychology itself. Under her influence Richard had attended a number of group encounters. One outcome was that Richard had begun to talk in a new way about my father, his thirteen years of marriage and many other things – including his fairly recent purchase of several Persian rugs

– which he now reckoned he had done only to please the old man. Tim disapproved of these confessions, but I found Richard's verbal gush a welcome change from the grunts and throat-clearings of the past.

Richard had become friendly and relaxed at last. We had dinner together and talked into the small hours. 'Everyone says you've landed on your feet,' I told him. Another time I boasted that I had just eaten a pot of caviar and he prised open my mouth to see the stains which could confirm my story. Again and again, Richard pledged his affection. In the early hours of one morning he woke me by banging on my basement door, dressed only in a pair of underpants and explaining that while putting the rubbish out, the door of his flat had slammed in his face.

My dealings with Edward were more distant and still mainly conducted in business jargon, though he would sometimes ring me out of the blue, informing me that it was a 'crispy' morning in Hong Kong, or at other times, drunk with success after a big business dinner party. His periodic visits to England continued, though I did not usually see much of him – and did not always know the time of his arrival.

One autumn morning in 1978, he rang me from Heathrow after a twenty-seven-hour delay to his flight, a misfortune to which he added characteristic embroidery. 'The capt'n fainted,' he told me in his mock West Country accent. 'I 'ad to bring the plane down moi-self.'

An hour later he arrived at my basement carrying a grocery bag from which he quickly drank two pints of milk, while I gazed with fascination at his great trousered pelvis.

After this cosy beginning I saw little of him. One of the purposes of the visit, apart from seeing my father, was to choose a preparatory school for his son, Toby, now eight years old. Mother and son followed him to England a few days later and we all met in a hamburger bar. Toby was small, bright, curly-headed and cheerful though at one moment he remarked, 'I wish I had a brother. You've got millions.'

The little boy had then fallen asleep and Edward had nodded in his direction, 'Out for the count!' and gone on to talk about my father, who he now suspected was 'guilty of gross misman-agement of the family's finances'.

Most of my meetings with Edward were more formal, squeezed in between business appointments, while my deal-ings with my sister-in-law were formalised by her habit of giving me on each occasion a beautifully wrapped gift. My last meeting with Edward took place over breakfast in a hotel and was marred by his spotting at another table a colleague from the Far East, whom he greeted with the words 'Hello there!'

20

It soon became obvious that my father's relationship with the Wiltshire widow was floundering.

'Matters have come to a pass,' he began biblically the next time he was in London. 'That is to say, June has made certain decisions. Having been to stay with me on the island for a week, she is obviously not prepared to come and live there as my wife. She talks about it as a mutual decision. Now the other thing is that having made that decision, she may have very great reservations against accepting me as a husband in Wiltshire and she may well decide to move out of this friend-ship altogether. And that I find very painful indeed.'

This doleful monologue ended with him saying, 'I've taken

a terrible knock, William,' and adding, 'Now she says I don't think we ought to telephone quite as much. I've written to her and said "Can I telephone you once every other month?"'

*

It was in these circumstances, and while still awaiting a reply to this letter, that my father suffered his second stroke. This time he remained in bed for several days, but when he got up he made light of what had occurred and his recovery again appeared total.

At Christmas 1978 I found him in high spirits, tap-dancing and even attempting high kicks in the kitchen, partly to frighten me, though I noticed that concern with his health had now replaced the question of re-marriage as his primary interest. The neighbours who now excited him most were those with medical connections.

'D'you know we have the greatest jaw surgeon in the world living here, Mr Sutton Taylor?'

He dwelt with glee on the circumstances of his second stroke – 'I woke up with the entire part-time staff of this place around my bed' – and blamed it partly on the tablets he had been taking. 'Every now and then you can get a rogue pill.'

He began to count the blessings of the island – 'The hospital here is just as good as the one in Bath' – and to look upon June in a new way – 'If I was ill, could she look after me? Has she had nursing experience?' – and he now began to find other faults in the woman he had once been so keen on. 'She loves talking to me about the Dockington estate but it's only about a third of the size of Jack Knife's place here.' He also claimed he had no rivals in his claims for June's affections. 'June is – she hasn't told me – seventy-three. She's obviously got no one else.'

To my surprise, my father had found someone else, an alternative to June in the shape of a Shropshire woman named Jennifer, whom he had known slightly for nearly fifty years. From time to time he would talk cryptically about these two, playing them off each other in his mind, and always sounding as if the decision about whom to marry was entirely his.

'This other party is of course much better off. I would make a decision in favour of Shropshire if only Shropshire had another twenty per cent. If only Shropshire had a sense of humour.'

I was relieved that he was also talking in more practical terms about the possibility of converting one of the outbuildings into a house for a caretaker couple and had taken the precaution of 'putting Mrs Quiggin on the phone', in other words paying for a telephone to be installed at the cleaning lady's cottage.

He was also willing to consider more remote accommodation possibilities. These ranged from 'a small furnished flat with every possible convenience in Frinton' to a place in a private nursing home. 'You pay Matron ten or fifteen thousand pounds and then you settle in.' Though he still studied the London Atlas regularly and it often lay open on his lap during his monologues, he now ruled out the possibility of living there. 'Do you really think that a man of my age living alone in London is anything but a pathetic spectacle?' he asked.

Our life together that Christmas fell into its familiar pattern. The only innovation was that the faithful Labrador was now shut each night into a distant garden shed – also housing the rusty remains of the Rover – because my father feared being woken by early morning barking. The sacredness of his sleep had been a lifelong preoccupation and the obsession was now highly developed.

In the kitchen, I took charge as usual – I noted with interest the panel of new linoleum which had been inserted where June had had a mishap with a burning tea towel – but this year my cooking failed to please my father. When I presented him with the usual turkey platter on Christmas Day, he said, 'I'm bored with turkey.' He preferred to try to cook his own meals, tinned and packet soups, frozen things, which he always secretly considered superior to proper food. These first attempts at cooking at the age of seventy-one were far from successful. 'Look here, William, there's a smell of—' he said, bolting back to the stove, and when he finally tasted some soup he tried to heat, bit upon something hard and dehydrated, 'Aaaagh!' he said irritably. ''Tisn't right. Must go back for more.'

My present to him this year was the book that I had now published but he showed only marginal interest in it, leafing through it briefly and consigning it to a side table. It was equally difficult to get him interested in any television programmes. 'Oh, look, Father,' I said as Sleeping Beauty was wheeled forward in a Christmas Day pantomime.

'I don't want to look,' he replied. 'I'm looking for a telephone number.'

He rustled about on the other side of the fireplace and then started dialling.

'Do you mind?' he said. 'Turning it off? Mrs Harris? Is that Mrs Harris? Oh, Mr Harris? What time is the service in the chapel tonight?'

As we set off together later, my father explained that he had fallen out with the vicar and joined with the local Methodists instead.

'The church would be unspeakable tonight anyway.' he added.

Ten other adults and an organist were gathered in the well-heated little chapel and they welcomed my father with real affection. Towards the end of the service, members of the congregation were invited to choose their favourite hymn.

Suddenly Mr Harris turned to my father. 'Do you have a favourite hymn, sir?'

For a moment I wondered if my father had the name of any hymn on the tip of his tongue but he proved equal to the challenge.

'We've just heard it,' he replied solemnly.

On the way home my father remarked, 'I've gone back to square one. Ended up where I started.'

He remained in a reflective and self-effacing mood when we got back to the house. 'I always used to snigger when I heard someone had had a stroke. Now when I told Jack Knife I had had a stroke, I thought he was sniggering.'

*

That evening, I was on the point of dishing up some supper when my father surprised me by placing a telephone call to Aunt Peg, who was celebrating Christmas alone in her cottage. He was now full of goodwill to his sister-in-law, and that night talked to her mainly about his stroke, the pills he had been taking – 'They are supposed to stop me having any sort of cerebral block' – and about the background of the doctor who was looking after him – 'He's a multiple butcher's son.'

'Thank you for your sympathy, Peg,' he said finally. 'I don't want any more of these things but I've got to expect them. Oh, Peg, you'll be interested. Your old parish council have accepted from me the gift of a specimen – probably a sycamore tree, in memory of Granny. I've tried to dissuade them from planting a copper beech.'

This placidity could not last and, sure enough, the nervousness returned and he began harping on again about 'this mental tie up I'm in . . . Mother's death and then this affair with June . . . I haven't a friend here, that's the honest answer.'

He became lost in melancholy. Finally he asked, 'What am I going to do, William?'

This sadness – 'I wouldn't mind being buried in Dockington churchyard' – was later eclipsed by anxiety about some dishcloths which kept going missing. This saga continued for the remainder of the visit, one cloth being missing and then another, and was followed by more dramatic imagined losses.

At tea-time on Boxing Day I was asked the whereabouts of a silver jug.

'Your guess is as good as mine, dear Father.'

'Wonderful boy!' he responded. 'A big inheritance under the will.'

The following morning he discovered that the lawnmower was missing from its shed. I could not help him about this either and after two hours of mounting suspense and suspicion, Mrs Quiggin came and whispered that my father was on the point of calling the police. Then, in the nick of time, he remembered that the machine was being repaired at the local garage.

*

On the eve of my departure, he fired a number of weird questions at me. 'Have you ever thought of undertaking as a business?' was followed by 'Would you like me to give you a salt-and-water enema?' As always I tried to steer him on to more serious topics, asking him, 'Do you believe in God, Father?'

This drew a somewhat testy reply from him, 'Now why do you ask that? I always have.'

Again he had bits of serious advice to offer me: 'It doesn't pay in life to be an oddster' and 'Don't marry a rich woman unless you can't find anybody else.'

He later showed off his independence by making a number of telephone calls to various neighbours. After two or three of these I suggested we rang Richard, but he wouldn't hear of it. 'Richard?' he mocked. 'D'you think he'd be any good at this hour?' and pressed on with local calls.

'Detective Sergeant Salter? Good evening, sir!' he began jauntily and went on to invite this neighbour to take a Christmas walk over his property – 'anywhere you like.'

He then telephoned the wife of the farmer who kept geese in one of his fields and discussed their drinking arrangements. 'They're now mature animals and they're taking a lot of water. Jolly good.'

With these and others he also discussed his health – 'Then of course my blood pressure went up like a rocket' – but it was always he who did most of the talking.

He was most at ease when gossiping with women. 'Miss McGinty? Oh tell me. Have you come across the baronet who lives near here – Sir Fergus Loft? There's always a good deal of mischief-making on the island but – I like him very much indeed. Of course it is very difficult indeed if you get a man who drinks very heavily and expects you to drink with him . . .'

Then his face puckered as he braced himself to make a final call, but he was soon chattering to yet another acquaintance about his life and health – 'I was in Oxford last month. Having a pair of trousers made' – and then finally accepting an invitation to lunch the following week. 'Like to come very much indeed,' he said. 'Are you sure it isn't my turn to entertain you?'

It was only after he had replaced the phone that I realised he had been talking to his old enemy Parker.

That night, shortly before midnight, my father tapped lightly on my door and said, 'May I come into your bedroom and smoke a cigar?'

'You're more than welcome,' I replied.

The following morning I left the house at ten past seven and my father did not get up to say goodbye. The icy side roads claimed the taxi-driver's full attention. 'I'll start talking when I'm on the main road,' he promised.

*

The end came quicker than anyone expected. Two months later, at the end of February, Tim telephoned me from the Isle of Man where he was doing his stint as a weekend guest. So often the bringer of bad news, Tim told me that my father had been taken to the Cottage Hospital at Ramsey.

'His heart is in a bad way' said Tim.

I was on the point of leaving for a holiday in France with the girl I was later to marry, but Tim was sure I need not postpone my trip. Five days later, a child came to the door of my rented cottage with a telegram, the contents of which it was not impossible to guess. 'Father died peacefully this morning Tuesday. Funeral Monday 12th March but try to be here Sunday when Edward arrives. Love Richard.'

For a moment or two, I gazed into the blazing log fire I had just lit.

*

I found my three surviving brothers already at the house, looking fresh-faced and sheepish, and also Catherine, the only woman present, who said she was convinced my father had died of a broken heart.

The windows had been opened, my father's office unlocked and the filing cabinet containing his scrupulously fair will had been opened. The money-oriented discussion was led by Richard and Edward. Richard had already had the house inspected and valued by an estate agent. Edward's bony fingers clasped a pocket calculator. I pretended to be bored by their deliberations.

'We all know examples of money not making people happy,' I said primly.

Edward laughed politely.

My father's body had already been cremated. At the funeral the following day, the Welsh taxi-driver carried his former passenger's ashes to the altar. Mr Parker, Mrs Whittle and several members of the Methodist community were among the mourners, and the service was conducted by the vicar with whom my father had fallen out ten months earlier, and presided over by the Bishop of Sodor and Man.

The presence of the island's ruling cleric was a mystery to us all. The bishop had never met or heard of my father or his family and when he came to give his makeshift funeral address and describe the glorious careers of my father's sons, he caused a certain amount of consternation by describing Richard as 'a publisher' and Tim as 'an architect'.

Aunt Peg was not present and the only mourner outside the family to come from England was my father's old accountant. I had not seen Mr Sweet for many years. He was now an old white-haired man, his head drooped but no poisons circulated his body.

'God bless you. Be good,' he said finally.

My brothers and I flew back to London together the following day. In his haste to return to his office, Richard left his briefcase on the carousel at Heathrow and had to return for it later.

THE END

ABOUT THE AUTHOR

Andrew Barrow is a former British journalist and author. He would regularly contribute to the pages of the *Independent*, the *Daily Telegraph* and the *Spectator*. Andrew's debut novel, *The Tap Dancer*, won the *McKitterick Prize* for best first novel by an author aged over 40, and the *Hawthornden Prize* for imaginative literature. He lives in London.